ILLUSION OF LOVE

Recent Titles by Denise Robins from Severn House

THE BITTER CORE
DEAR LOYALTY
THE GILDED CAGE
ILLUSION OF LOVE

ILLUSION OF LOVE

Denise Robins

This title first published in Great Britain 2000 by
SEVERN HOUSE PUBLISHERS LTD of
9–15 High Street, Sutton, Surrey SM1 1DF.
First published 1924 by Hodder & Stoughton Ltd.,
under the title *Sealed Lips.*
This title first published in the USA 2000 by
SEVERN HOUSE PUBLISHERS INC of
595 Madison Avenue, New York, N.Y. 10022.

British Library Cataloguing in Publication Data

Robins, Denise, 1897-1985
Illusion of love
1. Deception - Fiction
2. Love stories
I. Title
823.9'12 [F]

ISBN 0-7278-5577-8

Printed and bound in Great Britain by
MPG Books Ltd, Bodmin, Cornwall.

CHAPTER 1

June 1919

'If either of you know any impediment why ye may not be lawfully joined together in matrimony, ye do now confess it . . .'

The solemn charge, uttered in the low, sonorous voice of the officiating priest, echoed through the little church like a warning bell – then died away.

Silence followed.

Every eye was now focussed upon the young couple before the altar; the tall straight figure of the man; the slim, dainty form of the girl, who wore a biscuit-coloured lace frock; a wide-brimmed black hat on her golden head – an ostrich feather sweeping gracefully about the crown and curling down to her neck.

A slender girl in a blue costume – very shabby in comparison with the bride's smart toilet – occupied the front pew, quite alone.

She was the sister of the bride.

A few minutes ago her face had been pale, emotional, bathed in tears. She had been mother as well as sister to the bride ever since their parents had died and left them alone in the world. She felt as though Pamela were her own child to-day – her child being taken away from her by this tall man, who was being bound to Pamela by God and man.

But when these significant, impressive words 'ye do now confess it,' were uttered, her whole expression altered. Her cheeks flushed scarlet. Her hands gripped the rail of the pew with a convulsive movement.

'Oh, God!' she said beneath her breath. 'Oh, God, grant

that there is nothing – *nothing* in the way of an impediment! Grant that Pamela's marriage to Geoffrey may, undeed, be lawful!'

A strange prayer – passionately uttered – a prayer that would not have sprung to her lips had she not feared that there was the shadow of a doubt about it – a shadow that had darkened the brightness of her mind ever since Pamela had become engaged to Geoffrey Raynes.

The breathless hush in the church was broken. The clergyman was speaking again – to Geoffrey.

'Wilt thou have this woman to be thy wedded wife?'

The ceremony went on. Nobody had answered to that solemn charge – nobody had confessed any impediment.

Stella Morris raised her head and looked through a mist of tears at her sister. Pamela had turned her head slightly, so that her charming profile was revealed. How lovely she was, Stella thought – a lovely child of nineteen – a gay, care-free, irresponsible child! And this was the second time she had been led to the altar in matrimony – the second time within a year!

Through the stained-glass window to the right of the altar, the sunlight slanted on to the bride and bridegroom – wrapping them in a gold and roseate mantle of living colour.

'If only Geoffrey knew about it,' Stella thought, her heart painfully jerking. 'If only Pam had not deceived him – not pretended that she was an unmarried girl! She has done wrong – she will be committing a sin when she signs the register. 'Pamela Morris.' She is Pamela *Eden* – Julian Eden's widow. . . . '

Widow! Stella suddenly shivered as the word crossed her mind. If she only were sure that Pamela were Julian's widow! If only . . . *but she was not sure* . . . Pamela was not sure. This marriage, to-day, was a fearful risk; a gamble with fate. And if the fears that so often chilled Stella were ever verified, it would be a terrible thing – terrible for all concerned.

Supposing Pamela were committing bigamy to-day! Supposing that Geoffrey Raynes – kind, clean-minded, lovable Geoffrey – were ever to learn that the Pamela he worshipped and looked upon as an innocent baby, had been married, just over twelve months ago, to Julian Eden, an officer in the R.A.F.!

And supposing Julian, who had met a flying accident and been presumed dead, should return to find Pamela married again – faithless – forgetting her love and her vows within one short year!

Stella tried to rivet her attention on the young couple before the altar; to listen to the words the clergyman was saying; to deaden conscience, and countenance the wrong Pam was doing Geoffrey in so deceiving him. But it was difficult. Stella was one of those frank natures which shrink from anything shady or disloyal. She adored her young sister – had forgiven all her faults and follies time after time; but she was anguished in this hour by the fear that Pamela might be called upon, one day, to pay the penalty of her faithlessness and her lies.

'I pronounce that they be Man and Wife together . . . ' the priest was saying in his low, clear voice.

Stella drew a long breath – opened her eyes again and looked at Pamela. The thing was done. Pamela was Geoffrey's wife. From henceforward she would be Mrs. Raynes; the past would be wiped out – forgotten.

Forgotten by Pamela – but not by Stella. She could never forget that day, a year ago, when Pamela had come to her, a black-edged letter in her hand, her face swollen with weeping, and sobbed out her piteous confession.

A month previous to that, she had become acquainted with a fascinating young airman – the son and heir of Sir Richard and Lady Eden, who resided at Eden Hall, in Lyndhurst. He and Pamela – infatuated with each other – were secretly married at a registry office, on the fifteenth of June. Pam had been afraid to tell Stella, and he had not dare let his parents know that he had chosen an obscure little typist for his wife.

Three days after a stolen honeymoon, Julian had been sent on a world-flight in his aeroplane with a brother officer – Captain Horsman. He had promised that as soon as he came back, he would take Pamela down to Eden Hall.

He had never returned from that flight. The wreckage of his 'plane had been washed in to shore somewhere near Portugal and Captain Horsman's body with it. The body of the pilot – Captain Eden – had never been found, but he was reported 'missing – believed killed.'

A year had passed, bringing no word of him, so his young wife had presumed that he was dead.

Immediately after the fatality, Lady Eden had written to Pamela. She had been through her son's papers – found proof of his wedding to an unknown Miss Morris, who lived in London. Lady Eden wished to have nothing to do with her, neither would she make any provision for her. In answer to this cruel letter, Stella had written on her sister's behalf, proudly informing Lady Eden that Pamela would make no claims on her, but continue to earn her own living.

At first Stella had felt resentment in her heart against Julian for allowing Pamela to contract a secret marriage. But when she had seen his photograph – such a gay, boyish, winning face – she had forgiven him – just as she had forgiven Pamela her folly.

And now – a month ago – Pamela had met Geoffrey Raynes – a wealthy bachelor who had become acquainted with her at the big Insurance Office wherein both she and Stella worked as stenographers. And Pamela had forgotten that she had ever loved Julian so madly and passionately. She had wiped him right out – given her elastic heart to Geoffrey.

Stella believed that Pam really did care for Geoffrey – that he was her soul-mate as Julian Eden had never been. Poor Julian – so soon forgotten! Stella had begged her sister to wait awhile before marrying Geoffrey – wait – in case . . .

But Pamela had refused to wait, to admit that Julian might come back. And so here she was – married to Geoffrey. She had burnt her boats.

The ceremony came to an end. Stella followed the bride and bridegroom into the vestry, to sign the register. And now she made a valiant effort to control her emotion and conceal her fears – for Pamela's sake. Pam looked so radiant; Geoffrey's kind, handsome face was glowing with pride and happiness. Stella kissed them both.

'It's all too wonderful, Stella!' Pam whispered to her. 'I feel absolutely ecstatic.'

'God bless you, darling!' said Stella huskily. 'May nothing ever mar your ecstasy.'

'The only thing is that I shall hate leaving you when I go off to Paris this afternoon,' said Pamela with genuine feeling. 'You'll be all alone, Stella.'

'I shan't mind that,' said Stella bravely.

'You must hurry up and get married too,' said Pamela. 'There's Henry Waldon . . . '

Stella smiled a little. Poor Henry Waldon – the grave, rather heavy man, who had tried to woo and win her – in vain – for the last two years – and still vowed himself her suitor. He was one of the directors of the Insurance Company; and it would have been quite a good match. But not the match of Stella's dreams, neither was Henry Waldon the lover she desired.

'I shan't marry Henry – nor any man,' she told her sister. 'I haven't met the right one, Pam, darling.'

Half-an-hour later the sisters were in the bed-sitting-room in Kensal Rise, which they had shared for the last three years, in comparative happiness. Stella was on her knees before Pam's brand-new trunk, finishing the packing, and furtively wiping away her tears as she worked. Pam was changing from her delicate lace-gown into a fawn coat and skirt. She was flushed and very pretty – dimpling at her own reflection in the mirror as she placed a smart little feathered hat on her golden head.

Not a cloud on that charming baby-face; not a fear in that butterfly, inconsequent heart. It was Pamela's nature to be happy – and to cause unhappiness as she danced her way through life.

Stella was by far the finer character. Yet Stella had never had one-tenth the amusements or pleasure Pam had enjoyed.

She made a more beautiful picture than Pam, however – even in her simple clothes – as she knelt there beside the trunk, packing it with maternal care.

She was as dark as Pam was fair; smooth black hair plaited about a classical head; cream pale skin, with very faint colour save in the finely-moulded lips, which were naturally a deep red. She looked quite as young, although she was two years older than Pam. Despite the firm curve of chin and the steadfast expression of the wide grey eyes – there was something very youthful and appealing in Stella.

'I'm aching to see Paris, Stella,' came Pam's voice. 'Shan't I have some lovely frocks to bring back, eh? I'll bring you some, of course, darling.'

Stella rose and walked to her sister's side.

'Dear,' she said gently, 'I don't want beautiful frocks. I only want to know that you are happy – that you are going to be a good, faithful wife to Geoff.'

'I will,' said Pam – her blue eyes suddenly solemn. 'I swear it. I worship Geoff.'

'I believe that. It is why I let you marry him,' said Stella. 'But, oh, my dear – even now I wish you would tell him the truth – not deceive him and –'

'Nonsense,' interrupted Pam, sharply, drawing away from Stella's hand. 'It is impossible. He must never know.'

'Oh, Pam!' said Stella with sudden anguish in her voice. 'If Julian should not be dead – think – *think* – ' Pamela's face blanched. She bit her lip and put her left hand, with its new platinum wedding ring against her cheek.

'He won't come back – he's dead,' she muttered. 'Why do you want to spoil my wedding day?'

'I don't want to spoil it – only I'm so afraid sometimes,' said Stella breathlessly.

Somebody knocked at the door.

The landlady entered, grinning as she looked at the bride.

'Anyone here called Eden?' she asked.

Dead silence. Stella and Pamela exchanged queer, frightened glances. Then Stella said:

'Why, Mrs Smith?'

'Letter here for Mrs. Julian Eden,' said Mrs. Smith.

'Yes – that's – for me,' said Stella impulsively shielding Pam. 'Thank you, Mrs Smith.'

Mrs Smith looked at her curiously and departed.

'Who's it from?' broke out Pamela. 'Who has written to me – with – with *that* name?'

She had never used her first husband's name. She had called herself Pamela Morris since the day he had flown away.

Stella, the calmer of the two, ripped open the envelope. She had seen the postmark was 'Lyndhurst.'

'It's Lady Eden's handwriting,' she said tersely. 'Quick – read it with me, Pamela.'

Downstairs, Geoffrey Raynes waited for his bride – unconscious of the shadow that threatened his happiness.

Together, Stella and Pamela read what Julian Eden's mother had written.

'My dear Pamela,

'During this last year I have been thinking a great deal of my darling, dead son and the folly of his secret marriage to you. When I first learned of that marriage I was bitter and angry. But since then I have learned to bury my anger and to think more kindly of the girl my son made his wife.

'Sir Richard – Julian's father – died a month ago. I am a lonely woman and far from strong. I have thought, perhaps, that Julian would not have deceived me over his marriage had I been less proud and worldly; he might have brought you to me at once and told me that he had married a typist. In a measure, therefore, I am to blame, and I now wish to make amends for my uncharitable letter to you a year ago. You loved him, dear, so try to forgive me and love me. I want you to come to me at once – make your home with me. Accept me as your mother, and I feel sure our dear Julian will look down from his Heaven and be happy.

'I am coming to London to-morrow afternoon in my car, to fetch you, as I know you will not refuse to forgive, and live with Julian's old mother.

'Till then – with every tender thought –

'Yours,

'Ceciley Eden.'

Stella and Pam finished reading this long missive – then looked at each other in silence. They were both pale – their hearts pounding.

'Good lord, what a catastrophe!' muttered Pamela. 'This to come now – now of all times!'

'I knew something would happen,' said Stella. 'I felt it.'

'Of course I can't— I shan't go to Lady Eden,' said Pamela. 'It's too late.'

'She arrives here this afternoon,' said Stella.

Pamela bit her lip. Then she flung back her head with a defiant gesture.

'Oh, well— I shall be gone with Geoff. You will have to see the old girl, Stella, and tell her I'm gone – and get rid of her.'

'But how?'

'Any way you like, so long as you don't tell her where I am. I'm not going to let Julian's mother step in at the last moment to make trouble between Geoff and me.'

'But Pam!' said Stella. 'Am I to tell Lady Eden you have married again?'

'Why is that necessary? Simply say I'm abroad. Oh, say

anything, so long as she goes away and doesn't make trouble.'

Stella clasped her hands tightly together. Her beautiful face was puckered with worry.

'Pam, this seems all wrong,' she said. 'Really, you ought to make a clean breast of things with Geoff and Lady Eden.'

'Are you mad, Stella?' broke out Pamela, hotly. 'Tell Geoff the truth *now* – lose all my happiness – go down to Eden Hall and act the mourning widow for the rest of my life? No – no – never!'

A long silence. Stella's head ached with thought.

Then Pamela picked up Lady Eden's letter, laughed – and pitched it into the grate.

'That's it,' she said, shrugging her shoulders. 'When my lady comes this afternoon, Stella, you must see her and send her home again.'

Stella looked at her sister sadly, anxiously.

'I'll do whatever I can to help you, Pam,' she said. 'But, my dear, have you no heart at all – no feelings for that poor, lonely old woman?'

'No – none,' said Pamela. 'She deserves to be lonely. She ignored me when she first learned of Julian's marriage. Now she has swung round because she is getting old and lonely and wants me. Well – she won't get me.

Stella drew a long sigh.

'Oh, well, I'll have to go through with it,' she said. 'Lady Eden will be very surprised not to find you here, though. What had I better tell her? That you have married again – or not?'

Pamela was dusting her nose with powder now – smiling at her charming reflection in the mirror.

'Oh – just as you like, Stella,' she said airily. 'If the old girl has a weak heart, it might be too great a shock for her to learn that I'm married again, so if I were you, I'd keep it quiet, and just say I'm abroad.'

'I dread having to see her,' said Stella. 'She doesn't know about me – I don't suppose Julian ever bothered to say he had a sister-in-law, since he never met me, himself.'

'Perhaps, she'll take you for me,' said Pamela with a short laugh. 'Well, if she did, it wouldn't matter. You might go down to Eden Hall as the mourning widow and enjoy acting the part.'

'Don't be silly, Pam.' said her sister.

Later, however, those joking words were to be remembered – very seriously – by Stella.

Just now she felt that her head was in a whirl. Pam was Mrs. Geoffrey Raynes, just about to go away and leave her. Lady Eden was coming here in a few hours time to see her son's widow – and would find her gone. Geoffrey did not know the truth and . . . but Stella allowed her thoughts to carry her no further. She dared not . . .

She pushed the dark heavy hair back from her hot forehead and knelt by Pam's trunk again, to finish the packing.

A deep, happy voice came from the outside.

'Hurry up, you two! I want my baby-wife.'

'All right, Geoffrey,' Stella called back. 'She'll be ready in a moment, you impatient man.'

'You see how he loves me,' said Pamela happily. 'And I adore him. Not all the Lady Edens in the world could be allowed to separate us now, Stella.'

'Pray God nothing will ever happen to hurt either of you,' said Stella in a voice that betrayed her uneasiness. 'Pray God you will always be as happy as you are to-day.'

A few minutes later Stella was alone.

The sister who had shared her woes, work and pleasure, since their babyhood, had left her – departed on her honeymoon as Mrs. Geoffrey Raynes.

Stella was left to untangle the skein of follies and lies that Pam had left behind her.

'I wonder what I shall say to Lady Eden when she comes this afternoon,' Stella asked herself a dozen times, as she sat alone in the sitting-room, after the departure of the happy pair.

She was wretchedly lonely and depressed. She felt that she had nothing in life to look forward to, now that her beloved sister had gone. Love, light, warm vital happiness such as Pam was experiencing to-day – all these things were denied her, Stella. Life was very hard; and the joys of this world were very unevenly distributed.

Stella was in a nervous emotional condition quite foreign to her, when Lady Eden called to see Pamela that afternoon.

Stella faced her in the sitting-room, feeling utterly at a loss for words. She could only look at her. And as she looked, a deep pity for Julian's mother stole over her. Lady Eden was old and frail; her small body, so slight, so shrunken, it appeared as though a breath of wind could carry her away. Her face was deeply lined; her hair beautiful – white and waving. Her eyes were full of sadness. She had the expression of one who had suffered much.

She stared back at Stella, leaning on the ebony stick with which she had walked from the car.

Then, unexpectedly, she said:

'So you are my son's wife.'

The words gave Stella a shock. She stood there silent, flushing and paling under the scrutiny of the old lady's sorrowful, searching eyes. She felt herself trembling with cold nervousness. She tried to deny the statement – and no words came.

'So you are my son's wife,' repeated Lady Eden. 'Well, now that I see you I cannot wonder that Julian loved you. You are very beautiful, Pamela.'

Stella put a hand to her throat. To be called 'Pamela' was strange; to be looked upon as the wife of a dead airman, uncanny. She felt as though this were a dream; she was making an effort to deny that she was Julian's wife – and could not utter one word.

Lady Eden's delicate, ivory-tinted face was very kindly. If she had been hard in the past, she had obviously made up her mind now to atone for her harshness.

'My dear,' she said – her voice shook a little – 'we both loved Julian. I miss him unspeakably still. He was a fine, good, splendid boy. I was wrong, very wrong, not to take you to my heart in the beginning. Forgive me, child. Forgive me and come back to Eden Hall with me. Let us love and console each other – for his loss.'

Stella was scarlet now.

'But – but, Lady Eden,' she began, 'I am – '

'Don't say you will not come,' interrupted Julian's mother. 'Wait! Before you refuse, I will tell you something that may soften your heart toward me . . . '

Stella saw that the frail old body was shaking. At once she stepped forward and offered a chair to Lady Eden, who sank into it.

'Than you, child,' she said. 'I am not young, and the long drive from Lyndhurst has tired me out. But I had to come – for two big reasons. First of all I wanted to see you, and ask you to come home with me. Secondly I came to interview Sir Thomas Mander – the big heart-specialist in Harley Street.'

'Are you ill?' asked Stella, quickly sympathetic.

'I have not long to live,' said Lady Eden, with a sad little smile that went to Stella's heart. 'Sir Thomas has given me a few months – perhaps less than that.'

'Oh!' said Stella. 'I am sorry – so sorry.'

Lady Eden looked up into the lovely, grey, compassionate eyes of the girl she believed to be Julian's widow.

'If you are sorry, come back to Eden Hall with me, child,' she said brokenly. 'I need you and your love. I have nobody now. I may only live a few months. Won't you make those months happy ones for me – by being a real daughter to me? I have no husband – no son – only you – my son's wife. Pamela, I beg of you – come to me, please!'

Stella was silent. Her heart was violently beating. A dozen conflicting emotions were gripping her. And she thought of the words that Pamela had spoken in jest: 'Perhaps she'll take you for me . . . if she did it *wouldn't matter* . . . you might go down to Eden Hall . . . '

Those words had far more significance now. Lady Eden *had* mistaken her for Pamela, and was imploring her to go down to Eden Hall. She was old – infirm – she had only a few more months in which to live . . . .

Why should she, Stella, not let Lady Eden remain in happy ignorance of the truth – pretend to be Pamela – go with her to Lyndhurst to-day?

Perhaps if the old lady were to learn of Pamela's second marriage – realise that her last hope of happiness had gone – it would hasten her to the grave.

'My dear, don't refuse,' Stella heard Lady Eden's quivering voice. 'Ah, look at me, tell me you will try to love me and comfort me – just until – the end!'

Stella looked at her; saw that the proud old face was streaming with tears. And suddenly something seemed to snap in her heart. She flung herself on the ground at Lady Eden's feet, and pressing her face on the old lady's lap heard her own voice, as from a distance, husky, sobbing:

'Don't cry – don't cry. Yes, I will come with you and comfort you. I am lonely too. I need love and comfort. I will come, only please, please don't cry . . . !'

CHAPTER 2

That same afternoon Stella Morris motored back to Lyndhurst with Lady Eden, who believed her to be Pamela Eden.

How it all happened, and how it was finally arranged, Stella hardly knew. She was only conscious of the strange fact that she clung to Julian's mother; that she did not feel guilty or ashamed; but throbbing with emotion, with desire to love and comfort her. She felt as though by some miracle she had ceased to be Julian's sister-in-law, and become his widow.

In one short hour her existence as Stella Morris, typist, resident in a dreary lodging-house in Kensal Rise, ended – her new life as Mrs. Julian Eden began.

She did not go to the office. She dared not face Henry Waldon, who loved her and had wanted her for his wife. She wrote a cursory note saying that as Pamela was married she, Stella, was leaving London and 'going to stay with relatives,' and must give immediate notice to the office. She expected, of course, to forfeit her salary.

This done, she wired to the hotel in Paris at which Pamela and Geoffrey were to stay, and told them that she was going to Eden Hall.

As she had packed Julian's photograph in her trunk, she had whispered a few words to the pictured face.

'Forgive me, Julian,' she had said, 'Pamela has done you a wrong – I may be doing wrong. But I will try to be good to your mother. . . . '

When Lady Eden's car had left London well behind, on

its way to the New Forest, through Southampton, Stella felt utter relief. Already they were fringing the Forest. The glorious green and gold of it, after crowded, dusty London, brought tears to Stella's eyes.

Lady Eden saw the tears on the fine, dark lashes, and reached out a hand and covered the girl's.

'You are pleased to be with me – to get away from that hateful London?' she said. 'My dear! I understand.'

Stella laughed a little shakily.

'It is wonderful,' she said. 'I have never seen the New Forest before.'

'You must learn to look upon it as home. And you must look on me as your mother, child. I want you to call me 'mother.''

'Mother,' said Stella obediently. Her voice broke on the word. 'It will be wonderful to have a mother, too.'

Lady Eden squeezed her hand hard.

'I can't think why I didn't send for you before,' she said huskily. 'But somehow I didn't imagine Julian's Pamela – like you.'

Stella's cheeks coloured. She looked away at the cool, dim, spreading trees bordering the white hill up which the car was climbing.

Nothing more was said between them just then. A beautiful old Elizabethan house came into view; diamond-paned windows, like sheets of gold gleaming in the setting sun, between the dusky green leaves of the trees. Eden Hall! Julian's ancestral home; a fine old picturesque Tudor place with its old-world rose-garden and emerald lawns; the peaceful forest enclosing it on either side.

'Welcome to Eden Hall,' said Lady Eden. She bent and kissed Stella's cheek.

Stella hastily wiped her eyes as the car rolled up the drive. Emotion surged in her. She was not by nature foolishly sentimental, but this 'coming home' touched her beyond words. Away in Paris, Pamela was probably enjoying herself at Geoffrey Raynes' wife. Yet she was missing something fine and sweet – in all this.

The trial of being introduced to Julian's home was, however, greater than Stella anticipated, as the hours went by.

When they had finished tea, served in a beautiful, cool drawing-room where the window curtains were of pale violet silk, the walls panelled with rare old oak, the furniture antique – just the sort to satisfy the starved artist in Stella – Lady Eden took her over the whole house: showed her the old nursery, a cupboard full of broken toys, the cot that had been Julian's.

'I felt you would like to see these things,' she told Stella, leaning heavily on the girl's arm. 'He was a lovely, merry little boy – I will show you many photographs and snapshots of him later.'

Stella looked at the nursery, the toys, the faded relics of Julian's childhood, and bit her lip in her effort to control herself. Now, for the first time since leaving Kensal Rise, she felt ashamed . . . ashamed that she was deceiving the old woman who idolised Julian's memory.

Yet it was for Lady Eden's sake – for her sake more than for Pamela's. This revelation of the mother's love and grief for her dead son; the generous way in which she allowed her 'daughter-in-law' to pry into the sacred places and handle the sacred relics, filled Stella with shame. But it also knit her closely to the old woman. She felt now that it would be impossible to tell the disgraceful truth. Lady Eden already leaned on her for support in her grief; showed pathetic eagerness to share her memories of Julian with the girl he had made his wife.

'I am glad – glad you have come to be with me until the end,' she said, before she parted with Stella that night. 'You will make my last days happy ones – give me a daughter to take care of – and at the same time I feel I have someone to take care of me. You are strong and noble, Pamela – slender child though you are – I feel the strength of you. Julian must have felt it, too, when he fell in love with you.'

Stella averted her eyes.

And then Lady Eden said very wistfully:

'If only there had been a child – a son of my boy's – to help me to bear his loss – how wonderful that would have been. . . . '

Stella could not bear that. She broke down and ran to her bedroom. She did not see Lady Eden again that night. And Cecily Eden believed that the grey-eyed, dark-haired girl had loved Julian passionately, grieved for him as much to-day as she had done a year ago. Because of that, she knelt down at her bedside and prayed for forgiveness for ever having doubted Julian's wife.

But until late that night, Stella Morris, who was impersonating Pamela Eden, sat by her open casement and looked down at the moonlit garden, and beyond to the dark, tranquil woods, tortured with doubts – striving to make up her mind whether she would commit a great sin in remaining here under false pretences; or whether it would be a greater sin to ruin three lives – Pamela's – Geoffrey Raynes' trust in his wife – and perhaps to wreck the remaining few months of Lady Eden's life.

Of her own life, her own feelings, Stella did not think. She was so used to annihilating self.

'And, anyhow, it is too late to go back now,' she thought. 'I must go on – do what I can by helping and comforting Julian's mother.'

She looked round the exquisite little bedroom that had been given her. Its white walls; its pale rose-pink draperies and soft carpet were curiously virginal, youthful.

On the table at her bedside, Lady Eden had placed a photograph of Julian – Julian in graver mood than the one depicted in Pamela's photograph of him. Under this photo a crystal bowl of red roses spilled their fragrant loveliness, like an offering before a shrine.

Stella picked up the photograph and gazed at it, something akin to hunger, acute regret in her eyes.

CHAPTER 3

One week later Stella came down from her room, at seven o'clock, to join Lady Eden in the drawing-room for a quiet chat before dinner.

She had spent a glorious day riding the chestnut hunter which was one of Lady Eden's many generous gifts to her. Julian's mother could not do enough to show her affection and appreciation for her 'daughter-in-law'. And during that one short week, Stella had grown to love and admire the old lady; to speak of Julian without flushing guiltily; to take her place quietly and composedly as his widow.

A letter had come from Pamela, addressed to Mrs. Julian Eden:

'I am deliriously happy with Geoff. And I'm both amazed and delighted to know what you have done, Stella. You are a sport, after all, you dear funny old girl. It won't harm anyone. It will console Lady Eden, and it makes me relieved to know you are in such a comfortable home. . . . '

'It won't harm anyone' . . . those words had reiterated in Stella's mind. If only she could be sure . . . of that!

To-night, Stella made a charming picture in a pale grey chiffon frock which suited her dark, slender beauty. But her wide eyes were troubled. During the day Lady Eden had showed signs of increasing weakness. She refused to stay in bed or be treated as an invalid. But she was obviously very near the end that Stella had begun to dread.

Stella paused a moment outside the drawing-room door. She had heard Lady Eden's voice. Was there a visitor? Then suddenly an expression of horror, of amazement, crossed Stella's face. A man's deep voice was clear, comprehensible.

'Mother, darling, it means just as much to me as to you, to be home again, after a year's absolute hell. And it's simply wonderful news for me to know that Pamela is here, living with you.'

'Yes, dear – and she only came a week ago – long enough for me to have taken her right to my heart. She is a sweet, lovable girl, Julian. I thank God you chose her for your wife.'

Stella caught blindly at the handle of the door. The blood rushed to her cheeks. She knew at once that the unexpected had happened; the thunderbolt had fallen into this heaven of peace and rest. *Julian Eden had come back . . . from the dead . . .*

Julian's voice came again.

'I must go and find Pam,' he said. 'Oh, Mother, this is simply great! To be back here with the two I love best on earth – by Jove!'

'Wait here, Julian – I'll send her to you,' said Lady Eden. 'What a surprise for her, bless her heart! Well, well, joy never kills, or I'd have died when I looked upon your face to-night.'

'I didn't wire you,' he answered. 'I wanted it to be a surprise.'

Stella, still clinging to the door for support, now staggered a little to one side, and leaned against the walls, her cheeks deathly white.

The door opened. Lady Eden saw her and smiled – held out her hands.

'Pamela, my dear, dear girl – you have heard his voice – *yes*, I can see it. Isn't it too wonderful? God has answered all our prayers and our tears. Julian is alive. He was picked up from the wreckage by a tramp-steamer. For months he had been unable to remember his name or address, but suddenly, this summer, it all returned to him and so he has come home. He is changed, child – be prepared for a change. But he is my son – your husband – just the same. Go to him, Pamela – he is waiting for you.'

And before Stella could answer, she had been gently pushed into the drawing-room and the door closed behind her.

She found herself looking with dazed, terrified eyes at a tall man in a shabby, ill-fitting suit, who stood with his back to the fireplace.

He stared back at her.

She recognised him from his photographs: the fine features, the handsome eyes, and crisp, waving hair – as dark as her own. But he looked years older; and there were threads of white in the lock of hair that waved back from the forehead. Julian, the boy, had vanished. This was a man who had suffered.

A long, long moment passed. Then Julian Eden said:

'Who are you? My mother called you 'Pamela,' but you are not my wife.'

Stella put her hand against her heart. It beat so swiftly that it seemed to shake her slender body.

'I am – Stella,' she said, licking her dry lips, 'Pamela's sister.'

'Stella,' he repeated. 'Stella! Yes, I know Pamela had a sister, Stella. But why are you here, in her place? Where is my wife?'

Stella sat down helplessly. Her knees trembled so that she could no longer stand.

Julian Eden came across to her. He stood close to her.

'What has happened?' he asked roughly. 'Tell me at once. Where is my wife?'

'In Paris.'

'Paris? Why – *with whom?*'

Stella gulped and tried to answer without faltering.

'Captain Eden – I – don't know how to explain. It is all so awful – so unexpected. You were believed dead and –'

'I know; but what has happened to my wife? Tell me, for God's sake,' he said.

And so she told him. She told him the whole story – desperately – not daring to look at him – her hands locked in her lap.

Julian Eden stared down at her with incredulous eyes. His haggard face was as pale as hers – his lips twitching. It was an awful shock, that confession. His mother had told him that Pamela was here; loving, gentle, cherishing his memory. Instead, it was Pamela's sister. And Pamela was in France with another man – a man she had married a week ago. She had been so ready to forget; she had forgotten him within a year.

Julian had been through a little hell of his own since his plane had been wrecked and his brother officer killed, a year ago. He had gone through weeks and months of mental and physical agony, earning his bread-and-butter as a 'hand' on board the tramp-steamer, the captain of which was an uneducated Portuguese who had been willing to befriend the Englishman, but had no notion that England was searching for him, high and low.

Julian had improved slowly in bodily health, and months later, like a flash, his poor cramped brain had seen the light – he had remembered his name, all that had happened. That had been on the high seas many weeks ago. With agonising slowness (so it had seemed to him) the steamer had ploughed its way back to shore – and then he had found his way back to England.

He had gone straight to the lodgings in Kensal Rise wherein he had left his girl-bride. From the landlady he had learned that 'Mrs. Eden' had gone to Lyndhurst with Lady Eden a week ago. So he had rushed to the New Forest, eager, burning with love and longing for his wife.

His hands clenched at his sides. He looked at Stella with

a slow, scornful scrutiny that made her flinch.

'So!' he said. 'So my wife has forgotten me; I return like Enoch Arden, only at the end of one, instead of seven years – to find her re-married. And to make matters worse, you have dared impersonate her. Why? What were your reasons?'

'To comfort Lady Eden,' said Stella, scarlet to the roots of her hair. 'Yes – it was all for your mother's sake.'

'Or, perhaps for the sake of the home and money you thought you would get as my widow,' Julian sneered.

Stella sprang to her feet – quivering, stung to indignation.

'No – that is not true! I will go now – at once.'

Julian caught her wrist – stayed her.

'One moment,' he said. 'You can't go so fast. Remember, my mother is old and frail – indeed, I believe she is dying. . . . A second shock to-day – and an unpleasant one – would kill her. You came here and posed as my wife – you must pay the price of your deception of her. You aided and abetted my wife in wrong doing and –'

'No!' broke in Stella. 'No – I –'

'I say you did!' he broke in. 'I came here to-day thinking every sweet and tender thing possible of my wife – of all women. What you have told me has made me as bitter and contemptuous of your sex as I was the reverse.

'I – what are you going to do?' Stella gasped.

His blue, hard eyes looked her up and down.

'You are very beautiful,' he said, with a laugh that chilled her. 'Everybody in Eden Court believes you to be my wife. And I won't have my mother's last hours troubled, so now you shall go on with your game – carry it through. *You shall remain here as – my wife.'*

Stella was silent for a moment. Then she gave a short, nervous laugh.

'You must be mad,' she said. 'Remain here as your wife! – why, it is impossible!'

'Pardon me,' said Julian. 'It is possible, and it is going to be done. Remember that you, not I, started the game.'

'Yes, but I did not dream that you –' Stella broke off helplessly, her face hot and ashamed.

'That I was still alive,' he finished for her. 'No – quite so. But as I happen to have returned you must expect difficulties instead of the nice, clear pathway you mapped out for yourself.'

'You do me a great injustice by inferring that I impersonated your wife for the sake of a comfortable home,' said Stella hotly. 'I tell you that I came down to Eden Hall as – as your wife – for your mother's sake.'

'Very well,' said Julian. 'For my mother's sake you will remain here – as my wife. Until there is no longer any necessity,' he added significantly.

Stella felt her knees shaking. Suddenly she sat down – clasping her hands to her head – a head that ached and buzzed with feverish thought.

All the way along she had felt that this might happen; that Julian Eden might come back. In the church, during Pamela's wedding to Geoffrey Raynes, she had been in dread of it. Only during the last few days, in the beautiful peace and quiet of this home, the shadow of fear had slipped away. But now the ghost had come forward – assumed flesh. All her old fears were well-founded. Julian Eden was here – standing before her. She was believed by everybody in this house to be his wife. And his real wife, Pamela, was on her honeymoon in Paris, with Geoffrey.

'Oh! it's all horrible – unspeakable!' she broke out in a low, quivering voice. 'A ghastly mix-up – for us all.'

'You have only yourself to blame,' said Julian.

'And Pamela – do you blame her?'

Julian's face contracted. He bit his lower lip until the blood came.

'I loved her,' he said. 'I believed in her – felt positive she would be waiting for me. But she seemed only too ready to take it for granted that I died. It's only one year since she married me . . . and now . . . she's married to another fellow. My God!'

Stella looked up at him. The agony in his eyes, in his voice, drove all feelings save pity from her.

'Oh, poor Julian!' she cried.

It was the genuine, outspoken cry of her woman's heart. How many times in the past she had whispered those words, 'Poor Julian,' to his photograph, when she realised how little her sister had cared for him. Now that he was here, suffering, his faith, his pride, his love, all broken to pieces at her feet, she pitied him the more.

He stared down at her. The lovely, compassionate face in its frame of dark, soft hair, looked like the face of an angel. For months Julian Eden had been isolated from the world – had been veritably in hell. And Stella was the first young, attractive woman he had spoken to, for what seemed to him, long ages. But any softening influence her compassion and her beauty might have upon him, was swept away by the remembrance of his faithless young wife – this girl's own sister. Angel! Stella Morris was no angel. She was a scheming creature who had dared to impersonate Pamela, and he would punish her for it.

'I don't want your pity, thanks,' he said roughly. 'By the time I have finished, it will be you who will want pitying.'

Stella clenched her hands.

'You are determined to put a wrong construction on my actions, then – to condemn me utterly,' she said.

'You have done a very wrong thing,' he said. 'In coming here as my wife, you have not only deceived my mother but countenanced Pamela's wrong doing. Think of them,' he added between set teeth, 'in Paris – on their honey-moon. . . . My wife – and – another man! Curse them – curse them both!'

'Oh, don't,' said Stella in a choking voice.

'Pam is young and inconsequent, and – oh, try to forgive her. As for Geoffrey – he is one of the best men alive.'

'If he is a decent chap – I'm sorry for him,' said Julian. 'Apparently he has been duped – like I was.'

'Duped!' repeated Stella.

'Yes. Led into thinking Pamela a dear, innocent lovable child. She is not that. She is a worthless –'

'No, you are not to say terrible things of Pam,' broke in Stella. 'Whatever she has done, she is really only a child at heart. She found out that she had made a mistake when she married you. But she does care for Geoffrey Raynes. I know it.'

Julian gave a sneering laugh.

'I'm afraid I don't believe that. I shan't believe another word any woman tells me. And you have made things worse by posing as my wife.'

'I am terribly sorry,' she said. 'You won't believe it, but it is true. Your mother . . . ' her voice broke . . . 'was so pathetic when she came to see Pam. She needed love and sympathy. I – I gave it to her. I'm not sorry I did that.'

He looked at her, breathing quickly, his brows fiercely knit. He did not know whether to believe her or not. But anyhow he was not going to allow her to get out of things so easily, and hasten his mother to the grave.

'Look here,' he said. 'Whatever reasons you have had for coming here and impersonating Pamela, you must stick to the game now. I insist upon it. My mother apparently loves you and needs you. You've got to stay – until the tangle unravels itself.'

Stella rose to her feet.

'I can't stay. No – no!'

'You shall,' he said. 'You have *got* to stay.'

'The position would be intolerable,' she said. 'Out of the question. I must cable Pamela – let her know that you have returned. She must come back – at once.'

'How do you think that will affect my mother?' Julian flung at her. 'It is of my mother only that I am thinking, because she is the sweetest, finest woman on earth, and she is very close to the grave. I have already told you that another shock might kill her.'

Stella closed her eyes, striving desperately for clear, analytical thought. What Julian said was true. Lady Eden would not stand another shock. Besides, she must try to think of things from Pamela's standpoint, too. Pam had said on her wedding morning that nothing must ever part her from Geoffrey – that it would be the end of all things for her if anything happened to separate them. Poor Pamela! The news of Julian's home-coming would be a severe shock to her – to poor Geoffrey who loved her so.

'As far as I can see, everybody is going to suffer,' she said in a low voice.

'Except my mother,' said Julian. 'And I will not allow her to suffer. You must write to Pamela and tell her that I am alive – most certainly – but while mother lives she must be kept in ignorance of her daughter-in-law. When that is no longer necessary' his lips twitched slightly – 'then we must see what is to be done.'

She looked at him almost resentfully. He was being very hard. How he had changed! Even she, who had not known him personally, but had heard so much of him from his wife and mother, could perceive the alteration. The gay, sunny, charming boy had vanished forever. This man was bitter and relentless. Still handsome, still a magnetic personality, without a doubt – but as hard as nails. With a sick jerk of the heart, Stella remembered that it was Pam's infidelity and her own daring impersonation of Pam that had helped to make him what he was at this hour.

He came up to her and took her by the shoulders, looking down at her with those blue, compelling eyes of his.

'You understand,' he said in an authoritative tone.

'You will remain here as – my wife – until I choose to alter the situation.'

'You mean to enforce my obedience?' she asked, her slim figure stiffening in his hold.

'Yes, I do,' he said.

'And if I refuse – ?'

'You can't – you *daren't* refuse,' he said. 'Unless you want my mother's death at your door. . . . '

She shivered and the colour left her cheeks. She suddenly felt exhausted – unable to think or act for herself. Better to let Julian take command. She was swimming in deeper waters than she could manage.

'Very well,' she said wearily. 'I – I will stay.'

His hands fell away from her. He gave a sigh of relief.

'Thank you for so much!' he said shortly. 'And now I must ask you to pull yourself together and act your part without letting my mother dream there is anything wrong.'

Stella put up a hand and smoothed back her hair. She found her forehead damp and hot.

'I will – do my best,' she said. 'But I must write to Pamela. So must you.'

'I don't wish to,' he said. 'I could not possibly write one word. You must tell her. Tell her, too, that you are continuing your role for the present.'

'Yes,' said Stella.

He lit a cigarette, and glanced at her a moment over the cloud of smoke.

'We shall be forced to be polite to each other; perhaps more – to be affectionate – before my mother,' he said. 'But we shall both understand that it is acting on both sides.'

'Of course,' she forced.

As she returned his gaze a tremor went through her whole body. She could not forget the quiet hours she had spent in her room, wistful thoughts that had filled her mind; the strange, unaccountable longings that had possessed her for the love, the happiness that might have been hers – as his wife. She had become so closely knit with his mother; so familiar with the pictures and stories of his boyhood, that she had begun to feel a certain wistful tenderness towards him, despite the fact that she had no right to cherish his memory.

Now he was actually here – and she was to continue posing as his wife. She dreaded what she might be called upon to say, to do. And with the dread came intolerable shame because this man of whom she had thought with such tender pity looked upon her with scorn.

Julian opened the library door.

'Come,' he said. 'I think dinner is ready – and my mother will be waiting.'

CHAPTER 4

Dinner was over.

In the lovely mauve and silver drawing-room of Eden Hall, rosy with light from the silk-shaded hunterlites that stood in clusters of three in delicate brackets against the satin-panelled walls, Lady Eden lay on the sofa at right-angles to the fireplace.

As Julian and Stella joined her, she turned her head and smiled at them. She looked very happy, and her eyes were full of blissful contentment when they rested on the son who had been miraculously restored to her. But at the same time she looked very white and worn, as though the excitement of the reunion had sapped what little strength there had been in her frail body.

Stella's heart ached as she stood there beside the couch and saw the smile with which the mother greeted them both.

'Julian is right,' she thought. 'It would kill her to know the truth.'

'My darlings,' said Lady Eden. 'My two dear ones! Come and sit down beside me and talk to me.'

'Oughtn't you to be in bed, Mother?' asked Julian.

'In a moment I am going up, dear,' she replied, stretching out a hand to him. 'but I want to talk to you both for just a little while. It is wonderful to me to see you home Julian – with Pamela.'

He took her hand in both of his. But he did not answer. The name 'Pamela' jarred on him. And Stella sat down in an arm-chair by the couch, with her face averted. The sound of her sister's name had never distressed her more.

'Sit on the edge of Pamela's chair, Julian darling,' murmured Lady Eden. 'Let me see your arm around her. It does my tired eyes good to watch you lovers.'

Lovers! Stella felt a dry, hot sensation in her throat. She looked at Julian, then looked nervously away again. Not a muscle of his face moved. He had fine self-control.

Deliberately he sat down on the edge of her chair and put an arm around her. Her body quivered as she felt the pressure of that arm. It gave her almost a feeling of fear; it was so strong, so powerful – and absolutely passionless. In just such a way might he have enclasped a statue of marble.

'And what do you think of your little wife, Julian?' asked his mother. 'Do you think she looks very well?'

'First-rate,' said Julian, with admirable cheerfulness.

'You've no idea how fond I have become of her, bless her,' said Lady Eden. 'Ask her, and she will tell you that I have found a real daughter at last – just as I hope and believe she has found a mother in me.'

'You know that,' said Stella in a low voice.

She wished desperately that she could get up and rush from the room. She was overwrought and unequal to any display of emotion or demands of sentiment from her. It was all so farcical and at the same time so tragic. She could scarcely bear it.

Lady Eden continued speaking in that strain for several moments. She assured Julian that 'Pamela' was the sweetest girl in the world; that she deeply regretted that she had not met her in the first place and accepted her as a daughter-in-law before Sir Richard died.

'But now we must all three make up for lost time,' she ended. 'My last days on earth will be glorious ones – watching you two have a second honeymoon, here in Eden Hall.'

Stella made a movement as though to rise. Julian's arm, like steel, pressed her back in her chair. She bit her lip, fighting for composure.

'Yes, indeed, mother,' said Julian. 'And we will have a second honeymoon, won't we, dearest?' He turned to Stella. Looking up at him she saw that his eyes were grim. He had called her dearest, but – he hated her – despised her.

'Yes, I hope so, Julian,' she forced out.

'If you knew how she has grieved for you and prayed for you, my dear boy, you would realise how greatly you are loved,' said Lady Eden.

Julian's eyes narrowed. A tiny frown knit his brow. Grieved for him, prayed for him – this girl who was not his wife – who had never spoken to him before!

It was a wicked farce to pretend to mourn and pray. All for effect, or course.

Glancing down at her under his narrow lids, he saw her painfully flushing and paling. At least she was not graceless – shameless. She was obviously embarrassed by the situation.

At the same time Julian Eden's thoughts sped into another channel. He was a man of strong, primitive passions, and after this last year of mental torment, he had longed to hold his young wife in his arms. He had yearned to forget the terrible accident that had wrecked the plane, killed his brother-officer, and so nearly hurled him, Julian, into eternity, by burying his face in a soft silken cloud of hair; finding oblivion on warm, yielding lips.

He had come home to find his wife married to another man – and her sister in her place. This girl, Stella, was beautiful. Grudgingly he admitted that as he sat there on the arm of her chair, staring at her. He needed love. Why should he not demand it of Stella, who had dared to pose as his wife? Punish her – like that . . . '

His breath quickened. Stella saw a new gleam in the eyes that were vividly blue in the tanned, scarred face. Her heart gave a queer jerk. And the next moment what she had anticipated happened. He bent his head quickly and kissed her on the lips. It was not a light kiss. It was hard, deep, almost brutal in its intensity.

'My wife?' he said in a voice that his mother could hear. 'My darling, faithful wife!'

Stella did not reply. He had felt her slim body shiver – then grow taut during that kiss. And now, when he lifted his head again, he saw that she was trembling violently – deathly white. She sat back in the deep arm-chair – her eyes closed – struggling for self-possession.

She heard Lady Eden's soft, tired voice.

'Well, I am going to bed now. I will leave you dear lovers to yourselves. It is growing late. I don't suppose you will be long coming up. You look so tired, Julian darling – and no doubt Pamela is worn out with all this excitement.'

Julian rose and put an arm about his mother.

'We will come up with you,' he said. 'Won't we, darling?' he added, turning to Stella.

His words held a note of command to her. She resented it – yet she was forced to obey him. She was still tingling from head to foot with the memory of that hot kiss he had pressed on her lips. She looked at him in a helpless, terrified fashion. What did he mean to do now? Oh, surely the straight-living, kind-hearted boy of the past had not totally vanished and given place to a man without principles or mercy? She knew she had done wrong, but –

She dared think no further. In silence she walked out of the drawing-room and up the stairs with Lady Eden and Julian.

She opened the door of her own bedroom on the way. To her dismay she found that all her belongings had been taken out.

She turned to Lady Eden who, leaning on her son's arm, smiled gently at the girl.

'Yes, dear,' she nodded. 'I told Hannah to move your things to the spare room. Julian's have been put there, too.'

Scarlet to the roots of her hair, Stella looked at Julian –

silently appealing for support. But he only smiled in that grim way she was beginning to dread.

'Thanks awfully, Mother,' he said. 'I know that room it's jolly comfortable. Pam and I will be turning in now. Good night, dear.'

The mother kissed him tenderly. Then in turn she kissed Stella, who clung to her a moment, labouring under strong emotion.

The next moment Stella found herself alone in the passage with Julian. He took her arm firmly and led her to the spare room. As in a dream she went with him. She stared round her as he closed the door. The room was full of dim, rosy light from the electric light over the big Chippendale dressing-table. It was a lovely room, with soft primrose curtains and polished antique furniture. The windows were open, and a chink of pale moonlight slanted on to the deep gold-hued carpet. Stella's eyes travelled to the big double-bed with its white-lace bedspread turned back, showing snowy linen sheets, embroidered with the Eden monogram. She gave an hysterical little laugh and put both her hands up to her flaming cheeks.

'Of course this is – absurd, she gasped.

Julian came close to her.

'Is it absurd?' he asked in a low voice. 'You have pretended to be my wife. Why should you be surprised to find yourself here, in this room with me?'

She stepped back a pace, her heart pounding.

'I – it is a natural mistake on your mother's part,' she said. 'But you must go – or I must – as soon as everybody else is asleep. I can easily slip back into my former bedroom.'

'Indeed?' he said sarcastically. 'And when Hannah brings in your early morning cup of tea?'

'You will have to make some explanation,' said Stella. 'Say that you – you sleep badly since your accident and don't wish to disturb me, so – so – we – choose to have separate rooms!'

He looked at her – took in every detail of her appearance; the slender figure in the clinging grey frock; the bare creamy arms and throat; the flushed face with its wide grey eyes under dense black lashes, dilated with excitement – and fear. He saw the thick, dark ropes of her hair, plaited in a coronet about her head, and pictured that hair unbound – falling far below her waist like a dusky cloud. The vision seemed to go to his head, blotting out the memory of Pamela, his wife – the golden-haired, petulant child with whom he had thought himself so wildly in love.

He gripped Stella's slender hands in his and swung her into his arms. Like a vice he held her thus a moment.

'You are very lovely – very sweet to love. In spite of the wrong you have done in coming here as my wife I am disposed to forgive you – and keep you here,' he said in a low, hoarse voice. 'Do you understand – keep you here – with me. . . . '

She gave a gasping cry.

'Captain Eden – let me go! You must be mad!'

'You called me Julian a few moments ago,' he said. 'I am Julian – and I'm supposed to be your husband.'

'Let me go,' she repeated, white and shaking. 'Unless you want me to scream for help – disturb your mother – cause a terrible scandal!'

'You won't do that,' said Julian thickly. 'Look at me – kiss me – *my wife!*. . . .'

She tried to ward him off, but he imprisoned both her hands, and holding her tightly against him, set his lips to her mouth. It was a long, passionate kiss, robbing her of breath, of courage, of all her control. When he lifted his head, she broke down in his arms – sobbing pitifully, her head hidden on his breast – her whole body shaken with weeping.

Julian stood rigid. The passion left his eyes. He suddenly looked tired and very unhappy. The sound of Stella's sobbing seemed to unnerve him. He held her more gently as he looked down at the bowed head with its dark, tumbled hair.

'Oh, don't cry,' he said. His tone was rough, but no longer terrifying to her. 'I'm not going to hurt you. I'm not such a cad. For heaven's sake, stop crying! My mother may hear you.'

With an effort, Stella pulled herself together, and wiped her eyes. Conscious that she was still in Julian's arms, she gave a little shudder and drew away. She felt she hated him now – hated him for breaking her spirit. Whatever he did or said to her in the future she would show courage equal to his own.

She moved away from him, tilting her head in a pathetic effort to regain her pride.

'I will go – to my old room now,' she said. 'You can explain to Hannah.'

He had lit a cigarette. He did not move, but he looked inexpressibly weary, and the eyes that followed her were moody and bitter.

'Good night!' he said. 'I am sorry I – frightened you. But you must remember that your actions, as well as Pamela's, have helped to make me what I am.'

'I am sorry – too,' said Stella huskily. 'Good night!'

'Understand that we resume the relationship of husband and wife in the morning,' he added. 'Under no circumstances will I allow my mother to guess the truth.'

'I understand,' she said. 'Good night!'

She walked out of the room.

There was very little sleep for Julian that night. What sleep he gained was disturbed by memories of the girl who had posed as his wife, rather than of the wife who had proved so disloyal. He could not shut out the picture of Stella in her grey frock, in his arms, with her beautiful, terrified eyes gleaming at him, her lips shrinking under his kisses.

He wanted to despise her – punish her for the thing she had dared to do. He jeered at himself for being a weak fool to let her off so lightly, because she had broken down and cried. Yet she was so young, so much more beautiful in her dignified, womanly way than Pamela. No man could be a brute to her.

What to do now, he could not think. It was a horrible situation. But that his mother should be kept free from suspicion or worry, he was determined – at all costs.

In her own room, Stella spent a very similar night. Exhausted from her encounter with Julian, she lay in bed for long hours, wide-eyed, feverishly flushed, striving for calm thought. Her lips were bruised by his kisses; her arms ached where he had gripped and held her.

'He is a brute. I shall not stay here as his wife,' she told herself at one moment. And at the next she was pitying him. Poor, poor Julian! He had been wronged – deserted. He was half-mad with disappointment and worry. He was more to be pitied than blamed for his actions of to-night.

What a night it might have been for him – for Pamela. A wonderful, sacred night of love and reunion. Pamela had missed that; and he had been denied it. Poor Julian!

It was Stella's way to think of others more than herself. And when she did turn her thoughts to her own perilous position, she felt utterly confused; she could not see a clear pathway out of the maze of lies and deception. She could only wonder what would happen on the morrow; how long she would be forced to act her part as Mrs. Eden. It had been easy to pose as Julian's widow. As his wife it was far more difficult.

She awoke in the morning to fresh realisation of the tangled position, and the fact that she must act the part of Julian's wife again to-day. She would have run away had it not been for Lady Eden. She must never have it on her conscience that she had sent that sweet, frail woman to her grave.

She set her teeth and decided to 'carry on.'

She breakfasted alone. The butler told her that Captain Eden had taken an early meal, then gone out riding. She was thankful she was spared the embarrassment of the morning meal, *têtê-a-tête* with him. After a poor attempt at eating, she went up to Lady Eden's room.

The old lady, still in bed, greeted her with a happy smile.

'Ah, Pamela dear,' she said. 'How are you? I've already seen our darling boy. He told me you were still asleep, and so he left you because he longed for an early morning ride.'

'Yes, I – I know,' stammered Stella, with a scarlet flush.

'Bless him – he told me how happy he was,' murmured Lady Eden. 'And I can see that you are, too. You are like a shy bride, dear child, with your rosy cheeks.'

Rosy cheeks! Stella could have laughed had she not felt so much like weeping. She was thankful that her hot blush deceived the old lady.

'I'm feeling very much better,' Lady Eden observed. 'I suppose it is the joy of having Julian home again. I'm going to get Hannah to dress me now, and I shall sit in the garden. It is a perfect morning.'

'I'll see you down there, then, Mother dear,' said Stella. And fled – thankful to escape further conversation.

She walked into the garden feeling helpless. She had not written to Pamela yet. She dreaded the task of telling her sister the awful thing that had happened. The knowledge that her first husband was alive would shatter poor Pam's happiness – and Geoffrey's too. It made her second marriage illegal. It meant that Pam had committed *bigamy*. It was all too horrible.

She wandered through the garden toward the rosery, and sat down in an arbour that was a glorious tangle of purple clematis and climbing roses. She wanted to think – think in peace before Julian returned from his ride, and she must begin the struggle again.

How long she sat there, she did not know. But no clear thought came. And at last, with a tired sigh, she rose and walked back to the house.

Mid way across the lawn, she paused and stood stock-still, the colour draining from her cheeks, into which the sun had just kissed a warm glow.

There, outside the French windows of the dining-room, Lady Eden sat in her invalid's chair, covered with a light rug, and beside her a man was standing. It was not Julian, but a shorter man, with reddish-brown hair and a rather blunt, square face. Stella knew him – only too well. It was Henry Waldon – who had previously employed her in his office – the man who had been her faithful and persistent suitor for the last twelve months.

Her heart beat furiously as she saw him. Why had he followed her here? – and what was he saying to Lady Eden?

'Good heavens!' she thought, as she hurried toward them. 'Has he asked for *Miss Stella Morris?* Has he given the whole show away?'

For a moment Stella stood aghast, staring from Lady Eden to Henry Waldon. Then she realised that if she were going to avert a disaster, she must act swiftly.

She walked with rapid footsteps up to the pair. Waldon turned and saw her – his eyes lighting up. But before he could speak, she seized his arm.

'Henry!' she exclaimed. 'How good of you to come all this way to the New Forest to see me. I am delighted . . . .'

And then, turning to Lady Eden (from whose serene face Stella deducted at once, no harm had been done) she added:

'Mr. Waldon is my old friend and employer Mother dear. I am glad you have introduced yourselves. And now I'm going to carry him off for a chat.'

'Yes, do, dear,' said Lady Eden. 'He asked for Miss Morris when he first arrived, and seemed so surprised when he heard of your marriage to Julian.'

'*Miss* Morris – not Miss Stella Morris . . . ' thought the girl, trying to regain her calm. 'Thank goodness for that. Everything is all right. They have only just met – obviously'

Waldon had said nothing. He was staring at Stella with an expression of blank amazement on his face. This girl had worked for him for long months; had grown to be a dear and familiar figure in his office. He had always thought of her as one of the most quiet, reserved girls he had ever known. To-day she was a stranger to him – taking his arm and addressing him in this excited fashion. Her grey eyes were brilliant – her face crimson. What had happened? What was this all about?

Before he could question her, Stella had drawn him away from Lady Eden.

'There is a charming arbour down in the rosery,' she said. 'Come, we will sit there and talk.'

Once out of earshot of Julian's mother, her whole manner changed. Her face lost its vivid colour, and her eyes looked suddenly tired and dull.

Waldon found speech.

'My dear Stella!' he said. 'I'm afraid I don't understand all this business. I'm a bit bewildered.'

'Yes. I expect you are,' she said. 'I can quite understand it . . .' she gave a brief laugh . . . 'and I'm equally bewildered. It gave me an awful shock to see you standing there by Lady Eden. You are the last person I expected to see down here.'

'It needs a bit of explaining on both sides,' said Waldon slowly. They walked down the fragrant sunlit rosery and reached the cool arbour wherein Stella had been sitting a few moments before, alone. They sat down, while the man laid his hat aside and lit a cigarette. His deep-set eyes scrutinised her closely.

'Now, Stella,' he said. 'What on earth is the meaning of this? When I got your letter telling me you had gone to the New Forest to relatives, because Pamela was married and in France, I took the liberty of going to your old rooms to ask for your address. I wanted to see you again. I felt I could not let you go right out of my life. You know exactly how much I care for you . . . .'

Stella flushed and kept her eyes averted.

'Yes, I know, Henry. But, you know, also, that although I like and respect you, I have never given you any hope. . . .'

'Yes, quite so,' he broke in, frowning. 'But I thought you

might change your mind in time. I'm a good deal older than you are, and the sort of man who does not care for many women. You are the only one I've ever wanted to marry – and I have a good name, a good position to offer. So I considered I might follow you and – try my luck again.'

'I – see,' stammered Stella.

'However, when I spoke you your landlady, she gave me a mysterious account of your doings directly after your sister's marriage. She informed me that you were *married,* and that as 'Mrs. Julian Eden' you had accompanied your mother-in-law to Eden Hall, Lyndhurst. I was simply astounded. I came straight here to find out the truth. The maid took me to Lady Eden and I asked for Miss Morris and she said there was no Miss Morris here – only her son's wife, Mrs. Eden. Just as I was about to make further inquiries, you came . . . .'

'Thank heaven,' reflected Stella.

She looked at Waldon with a rather desperate expression in her eyes. She could not tell him the truth. She knew that he would create a hideous row if he thought for one moment she was only pretending to be Julian's wife. He was one of those strange, quiet, blunt men whose passions are strong and whose primeval instincts are apt to break very easily through the thin veneer of civilisation. He was madly in love with her. She was quite aware of the fact that it was no ordinary passion that had led him to follow her here. Therefore, she must be careful, and treat the situation with the utmost tact and delicacy.

So far all was well. He did not know that she was called 'Pamela' in this house. He had no cause to be suspicious. The best thing she could possibly do was get him out of the place as speedily as possible, before anything unforseen happened to arouse his suspicions.

'Listen, Henry,' she began in a low voice. 'I am very sorry I deceived you while I was working for you. To tell you the truth, I . . . I have been married for some time to Julian Eden.'

Waldon looked at her with an expression of deep resentment.

'Oh, Stella,' he said. 'Why did you keep it secret?'

With downcast eyes and burning cheeks she proceeded to tell him the story of the 'secret marriage'; of Julian's flying accident; of his mother's request that she should take her place at Eden Hall as his widow – and then his unexpected return.

Waldon listened moodily. At the end of the story he gave a mirthless laugh.

'That ends everything, then. You are this fellow's wife, and he has come back. My hopes are dead.'

Stella suddenly felt very sorry for him.

'I wish you did not feel – had never felt – like this about me. Henry,' she said. 'You have been such a good friend and a kind employer that I feel I have . . . .'

'Oh, please don't apologise,' he cut in roughly. 'You have only done me an injustice in allowing me to think of you as single.'

Stella was silent. She felt helpless. She had not done him that injustice. She was doing herself one in allowing him to believe it. But she could not explain.

'I shall be wrapped up in a hopeless tangle of lies before I've finished,' she told herself. 'It is unbearable.'

Waldon stood up, twisting his hat in his fingers. His square face was white in the sunlight, and the reddish-brown eyes were bitter.

'I'd better say good-bye,' he said.

Stella rose. She held out her hand.

'Good-bye, and forgive me, Henry,' she said. 'I'm dreadfully sorry about it all and believe me I do appreciate the impulse that led you to come all this way to see me.'

He looked at the slim, outstretched hand, then at the beautiful, slender figure in the tussore frock; the delicately-cut face in its frame of soft, dark hair – the grey, appealing eyes.

He had never loved nor wanted any woman as he loved

and wanted Stella. The cruelty of fate; the belief that another man had the wonderful gift of her love and her beauty, smote him like a blow, temporarily robbing him of control. He seized her hand and flung an arm around her.

'Oh, Stella. I love you so!' he groaned.

'Don't – you must not – please,' she stammered.

She bit her lip. It was quivering. Perhaps she had never realised till this moment quite how badly Henry Waldon had been hit. Although he was utterly unlike the lover of her dreams, although his touch had no power to stir her for the fraction of an instant, yet she liked him – had always admired his business capabilities, his generous, kindly nature.

She was sorry she had hurt him. And she felt a queer depression steal over her as she saw him put on his hat and turn to leave her. She was losing a good friend. She had no other friends in the world. She was alone, terribly alone – had he but known it; she was living hourly on the brink of a precipice. Lady Eden's loving affection heaped coals of fire on her head; Julian despised her and was making her pay a bitter price for her impersonation of his wife.

And now Henry Waldon would go back to town and she would never see him again.

Almost it was on the tip of her tongue to detain him, to pour out the whole truth, to throw herself on his mercy, beg him to help her out of the difficulties that were weighing her down.

But a dark shadow suddenly blotted out the sunlight from the arbour. She saw Julian Eden standing on the pathway, smiling at her. It was a smile that made her shiver. It was so ironical. How long had he been there? Had he been standing behind the bushes? Had he overheard the conversation between her and Henry Waldon?

She knew in a moment that he had. For he called her *Stella.* He desired to keep up appearances before Waldon.

'Hullo, Stella darling,' he said. Then to the man: 'I heard from my mother that you were here. An old friend of my wife's aren't you?'

'Yes, I am,' said Waldon stiffly.

The eyes of the two men met – clashed – each suspicious of the other, both antagonistic.

Stella watched them, one hand on her fast-beating heart. She could not help contrasting them – to Julian's advantage. He looked extraordinarily handsome, standing there in his well-cut riding clothes; soft collar and tie, and leather gaiters; his dark sleek head bared to the sunlight. He stood a good head taller than Waldon.

'If you were really my husband,' Stella thought. 'How proud I should be at this moment. And instead – I am ashamed.'

Julian walked lazily up to her and put an arm around her shoulder. His hands touched her bare neck, and she felt his fingers burn her flesh like fire.

'You'll stay to lunch, Waldon, I hope,' he said pleasantly.

'Thank you, no,' said Henry. 'I must be getting back to town.'

He threw another hostile glance at the man who had dared to marry Stella secretly, and had come back, more or less from the dead, to claim her. Then he looked at Stella. She was flushing and paling alternately, her slim figure in the circle of Julian's arm. She was, of course, in love with her husband.

Waldon's cup of bitterness seemed to overflow.

'Good-bye, Stella. Good-bye, Captain Eden,' he forced. He shook hands formally with them. 'I must – congratulate you both.'

Then he turned and walked swiftly away down the gravel path towards the drive.

CHAPTER 5

Julian's arm fell away from Stella.

He tapped his riding-crop against his boots, and looked at her inquiringly.

'And who is this Mr. Waldon who has come all the way to Lyndhurst to make love to you, may I ask?'

Stella flushed scarlet.

'He was – my employer – the head of the Insurance Company for which I worked.'

'I see. There was 'an affair' between you?'

'No. He – cared for me. I did not love him.'

'H'm, you were looking quite depressed when I saw you,' said Julian sarcastically. 'I thought perhaps you were in love with him.'

'No. I like him. I felt sorry he was going away with a wrong impression of me. That's all,' she said.

'You have only yourself to blame.'

'You delight in saying that,' she broke out, breathing fast. 'At every available opportunity I suppose you mean to remind me that the fault is mine.'

'It is only what you deserve,' he said.

'I am doing my best to – spare your mother any sorrow,' said the girl desperately. 'Why can't you be content with that? Or do you want to make me suffer more by making sarcastic, horrid remarks?'

Julian shrugged his shoulders.

'I'm afraid I haven't it in me to make pretty speeches to you, my dear Pamela. Yes, I must get into the habit of calling you 'Pamela' again. I noticed that Waldon was addressing you as Stella, so I took my cue.'

'It is fortunate that he did not give the whole game away to your mother,' said Stella with a tired sigh. 'I only came upon them just in time.'

'I'd have broken every bone in his body if he had upset Mother,' muttered Julian, with a dark scowl.

Stella's grey eyes regarded him for a moment, much as she might have regarded an unreasonable child.

'I don't consider it would have been Henry's fault if he *had* given the show away,' she said. 'He knows that I am Stella, and –'

'Oh, don't trouble to defend him. I'm sorry for the poor wretch,' broke in Julian with a brief laugh. 'Sorry he is in love with *you* . . . .'

Stella made a movement toward the garden path.

'I am not going to stay here to be insulted by you,' she said in a quivering voice. 'I think you are an absolute brute.'

'I daresay,' he said. 'As I said last night, I am what you and Pamela between you have made me. No, don't be in such a hurry,' he added, detaining her with a hand on her arm.

'What do you want?' She tilted her beautiful head.

Julian looked down into her eyes. His lips twitched slightly as he saw the pitifully troubled expression in them. A brute! Yes, he was a brute to her. Somehow he wanted to be. She had so completely upset his equilibrium – she, more than Pamela, his faithless wife. All last night had not his dreams been haunted by Stella?

He pulled her into his arms with a rough movement.

'You look charming in that silky gown,' he said. 'It suits you. It is the first time I have seen you this morning. My loving wife . . . won't you kiss me?'

'There is no need to act a part when we are alone,' she gasped, straining back from him. 'Please let me go.'

'When you have kissed me.'

'I will not. What right have you to ask me?'

'What right had you to pose as my wife?'

She looked up at him and saw his mocking, twisted smile.

'Oh, let me go,' she said. 'Don't be so cruel.'

'It is cruel of you to deny me your kisses. I am a lonely, hungry man, and I am only just beginning to *live* again.'

She tried to free herself from his imprisoning arms.

'Julian, be reasonable, for heaven's sake. Remember your – your wife – '

'I don't wish to remember her,' he broke in fiercely. 'Hasn't she robbed me of all that I had hoped for when I came rushing back to England this week? I want to forget her.'

'But you can't want to – kiss me,' said Stella in a desperate voice. 'You hate me.'

'And you hate me?'

She looked away from him, her heart pounding so that it shook her slender body.

'You will make me hate you – very soon,' she said in a choking voice.

'You do already. I know it.'

She was silent. He regarded her with his blue, cynical eyes for a moment. Then he bent and kissed her on the lips.

'This is your punishment, my dear,' he said when he raised his head again. 'I am a brute, as you say, and I find your lips very sweet to kiss.'

Stella was white – speechless. She wanted to hate him for his ruthless cruelty, his contempt. She knew that she *ought* to hate him. Yet the passionate grip of his hands and the burning pressure of his mouth roused all the responsive passion in her own body. She had loved the memory of the Julian who was dead . . . and now there rushed across her face the bitter-sweet knowledge that she loved the living Julian far more. It made the position all the more intolerable.

She covered her face with her hands and stood thus in

silence for a moment.

'I can't go on with this,' she thought. 'It is hopeless. I must write to Pamela and tell her she must help me out.

'You take things to heart,' she heard Julian's voice. 'I suppose you are in love with this Henry Waldon.'

Stella felt an hysterical desire to laugh. At the same time she registered a mental vow that Julian must never, never know the strange mixture of honey and gall that she tasted in the 'punishment' he meted out to her. She felt distressing shame at her own knowledge of her emotion. But under such emotion she was powerless. Love and passion are strong and merciless factors, beyond the control of poor human beings. Physical expression of them may be controlled, but to reckless thought there is no barrier.

'Supposing I am in love with Mr. Waldon,' she said. 'What does it matter to you?'

'It matters at the moment,' he said. 'You are in my wife's shoes.'

'I'm not allowed to forget that,' said Stella rather bitterly. 'All the same I owe you no fidelity.'

'Indeed?' His blue eyes narrowed to slits, and his firm lips tightened as he looked down at her flushed, rebellious face. 'We shall see. If Waldon had continued with his love-making just now, there would have been trouble.'

'Well, he didn't, and he won't come here again, so let us drop the subject,' said Stella wearily. 'I can promise you that I shall not be – unfaithful – while I bear the name of Mrs. Julian Eden.'

'Thanks for so much,' he said.

'I am going to the library now to write to Pamela,' said Stella, quietly.

Julian's whole face seemed to darken.

'Yes, it is just as well you should do so. I will remain in the garden with my mother until you have finished.'

'Do you wish to read what I write, since you are so much my lord and master?' she asked, with a quivering face that held no mirth.

'No. I leave it to you,' he said. 'But tell her that she need not expect to get off scot-free. She was faithless to me and she has deceived the man she has bigamously married. She will have to account for it all one day.'

Stella shivered.

'When my mother no longer lives,' added Julian in a low, curt voice. 'But until then, Pamela can go on her own sweet way, and you will remain with me.'

'It isn't right,' said Stella. 'Pam is living with Geoffrey in – in sin . . . and if . . . oh, can't you understand what a terrible thing it will be if . . . she has a child . . .'

A long silence followed this stammered speech. Out in the rose garden, two white butterflies chased each other over the flower-beds. A thrush was singing up in the branches of a dark green fir; and now and then there came the drowsy hum of a bee. Out there was beauty, peace, the fulfilment of summer.

In the arbour stood a man and a girl from whom peace was very far. Indeed, Stella felt she would never know the meaning of peace again. She saw that Julian had flushed deep red. His hands were clenched.

At last he broke the silence.

'What you suggest is true and might easily happen. If it does – there is only one way out of things. I must divorce Pamela.'

'But what about Geoffrey? You don't know him as I do. He has absolute belief in Pam's innocence and purity. He is not the modern stamp of man to whom divorce is a fashionable pastime. He would abhor the idea, and possibly refuse to entertain it. Then Pam – poor little Pam –' Stella's voice broke.

'I'm afraid I have no pity for her,' said Julian harshly. 'But in any case let us hope there will be no complications of that sort. Pam will realise when she gets your letter that there must be no children.'

'You mean to take her back – one day?'

'I don't know. I haven't definitely made up any plans,' he

said, tapping his riding-crop against his gaiters with a quick, nervous movement. 'At the moment I can't look a day ahead. My only thought is for mother.'

Stella drew a strangled sigh.

'I will write to Pam – now,' she said.

She moved away. He stood watching the slim figure go down the path toward the house. The slim shoulders drooped; the dark head was drooping too. She looked terribly tired.

Julian flung himself down on the wooden seat in the arbour and put his head between his hands.

'What a muddle! What a frightful muddle!' he said aloud.

And almost he wished he had died that day his aeroplane had crashed into the sea . . . died . . . and never come back to this home over which the very Sword of Damocles was suspended, waiting to sever the delicate thread of his beloved mother's life.

CHAPTER 6

One week later, Stella sat in the drawing-room with Lady Eden, reading a long letter from Pamela. It was as well, reflected the girl, that the old lady was peacefully reading her daily paper, and ignorant of the contents of that wild letter from Paris.

Stella's news had reached Pamela after a day or two's delay, since they had moved from one hotel to another. Of course, it had been a horrible shock, and for once the gay, inconsequent girl was startled into genuine fright and despair.

'When I first realised that Julian had come back – after all these months – I nearly committed suicide' (Pamela wrote). 'I can't believe it even now. Oh, Stella, for God's sake go on with your part. You have brought a good deal of trouble on yourself through giving way to your enormous sympathy for Lady Eden. Go on with what you have begun for MY sake now. I worship Geoffrey. Every day he grows more dear to me, and he would break his heart if he were to learn I had committed bigamy. How unspeakably cruel of fate to bring Julian back just as I had found happiness. Don't preach right and wrong to me, Stella, and say that I ought not to go on living with Geoffrey. I can't part from him now. I shall take care not to return to England – make Geoffrey keep me abroad. You must keep up appearances your end – until Lady Eden dies . . . .'

There was plenty more of the letter in this strain: all typical of the writer. Pamela looked at things from a totally selfish point of view. She feared for her own happiness.

She gave no thought to Stella's or her first husband's ghastly position.

Stella folded up the letter and sighed deeply. She looked wan and pale this afternoon. She had had little sleep lately. She had been worrying so. It was such a strain this 'keeping up appearances.' Julian was constantly by her side, making love to her before his mother – mocking her when they were alone. He was ruthless in his desire to 'make her pay.' How would it all end? She could not think.

She only knew that as the days went by things became more difficult to bear, because of her own conflicting emotions. To feel Julian's arms about her, or his kisses on her mouth, was torture now – because she loved him. Unreservedly, to herself, she admitted that. She loved him and suffered agony because he seemed to hate her and delight in inflicting torture on her. But far worse was the knowledge that he was her sister's husband – her *brother-in-law*. If only she could think of him as a brother, how much easier everything would be.

Stella needed an immense amount of self-control. She felt she would rather die than let Julian Eden dream that she cared – *that* way.

She looked through the window as she finished reading her letter from Pamela, and saw Julian strolling across the lawn. He wore flannels and a college blazer, and looked extraordinarily youthful to-day. His face was less haggard and worn, and he was growing sunburned. Except for that white lock of hair and the tiny network of lines about his mouth and eyes, he looked more like the old Julian of the photographs. Yet he could be so hard – so cruel!

Stella's heart contracted. Rising she went out on the sun-dappled lawn and joined him.

'Julian,' she said in a low tone. 'Here is Pamela's reply.'

He took the letter she handed him, read it through in silence, then returned it to her.

'Burn it right away,' he said brusquely. 'I have few comments to make. The whole thing is characteristic of her. Even in the days when I was madly in love with her I knew in my heart that Pamela was self-centred and callous. She thinks only of herself.'

'I don't know that you think of her at all,' said Stella in a low tone.

'I don't intend to,' he said, coolly lighting a cigarette. 'I am much too proud to waste any love or sympathy on a woman who has shown me neither.'

'What are we going to do now?'

'What your charming sister suggests. Keep up appearances . . . until my mother dies. . . .'

'How much more do you think *I* am going to be able to stand of this?' asked Stella bitterly.

'You've stood it well this week,' he said. 'You can carry on a bit longer, my dear.'

'I am between the devil and the deep sea,' she said with a dreary laugh.

The hoot-toot of a car made them both turn round toward the drive. A smart little two-seater, its single occupant being a man in a grey suit and soft hat, was coming up to Eden Hall.

'Who is this?' asked Stella.

'Oh, lord, muttered Julian. 'It's a cousin of mine and the last man on earth I wanted to see. His name's Basil Hargreaves, and he's a son of my mother's sister, Lady Hargreaves, who lives in Southampton.'

'Has he heard you are home, then?'

'Presumably. Mother, no doubt, wrote to Aunt Helen and blazoned the fact abroad. For heaven's sake don't make a slip – while Basil's here.'

Basil Hargreaves pulled up in the car, switched off his engine and came up to the couple on the lawn, hailing them cheerfully.

'Hullo, old man . . . ' to Julian. 'By Jove, it's good to see you again. We all thought you were gone for good. This the little wife Aunt Cecily's been writing about? Yards of the admiration stuff. I've been longing to meet her. . . .'

Julian made the introduction. Stella shook hands with Basil, trying to smile. But she felt cold and nervous, and she took an instant dislike to Julian's cousin. He was the antithesis of Julian; shorter and of slimmer build, and very fair. He had a pale, rather dissipated face, and hazel eyes, which rested on Stella altogether too boldly.

The three of them walked into the drawing-room.

Lady Eden greeted her nephew affectionately. She did not see him very often, and was quite ignorant of the fact that he was an indolent young roué who was breaking his mother's heart. Lady Hargreaves was loyal to her son and spoke well of him to 'the family.'

'I'm glad to see you, Basil,' said Lady Eden. 'So you've motored from Southampton, have you?'

'Yes, and brought my suit-case along. I say, Aunt Cecily, will you be an angel and put me up for the week-end?'

'Delighted, my dear boy,' said Lady Eden.

Julian exchanged glances with Stella, who looked dismayed.

'Shall I be spoiling things by staying, Cousin Pamela?' drawled Basil, with a side-long glance at the girl.

'Not a bit,' stammered Stella. 'But we – there isn't a spare room, is there, Mother?' she appealed to Lady Eden.

The old lady smiled at her.

'Yes, we can manage, my dear,' she said innocently. 'I'll give Basil that single bedroom of yours, and get Hannah to put two beds in Julian's big room. You two will have to share a room in the good old-fashioned way for the week-end. But I'm sure you won't mind.'

Complete silence followed this. Stella was scarlet to the roots of her hair. Julian bit savagely at his lip. And Basil Hargreaves, looking from one to another, raised his eyebrows.

'H'm . . . not all roses here,' he reflected shrewdly.

'What's up with the loving pair? Aren't they lovers after all?'

The curious expression in Basil Hargreaves' eyes warned Stella that she must bottle up her feelings at once and continue playing her part with composure, unless she wanted Julian's cousin to guess that something was wrong.

She pulled herself together and, with a great effort, smiled.

'Oh, of course, Mother,' she said, 'Julian and I won't mind moving our things again – will we, darling?' She turned to Julian, her heart beating violently, her face vividly flushed.

'Rather not,' he said, taking his cue. 'That'll be all right. You'll put up with us, Basil, I hope.'

'Oh, thanks, old chap,' drawled Basil. 'I'm delighted. Won't stay long, y'know; don't want to butt in when you've just come home.'

Julian thrust his hands into his pockets and stared at the carpet. He was still chewing at his lower lip, endeavouring to keep cool. Basil must be a fool not to see that he was 'butting in' now – very much. But there was nothing to be done, without raising suspicion. He would have to stay here the week-end.

Julian's pulses beat a little thickly, however, as he reviewed the situation. What on earth were he and Stella to do about this bedroom business now, he wondered? It was going to be awkward . . . deuced awkward. Not so easy to manage this time. . . .

When Stella had looked at him just now, he had been fully aware of her mental struggle. Her grey, appealing eyes were eloquent. After all, she was being very plucky. He wished those eyes of hers were not quite so beautiful and appealing. He wanted her to suffer and yet – if ever their eyes met – he felt a cur. That was all wrong. She had wickedly impersonated his wife. She deserved to be punished.

Yet how sweetly the word 'darling' had fallen from her lips. Her voice was so soft – so much more sympathetic than Pamela's high-pitched young voice had been.

The thought of Pamela helped to harden Julian again.

'I mustn't be an infernal idiot,' he told himself savagely. 'Whatever happend, Stella has brought it on herself, and I'm not in the least sorry for her.'

'Julian, old chap, your wife is not in the least what I expected her to be like,' Basil Hargreaves was saying.

'Why?' grunted Julian.

'Oh, I dunno. Somehow I conjured up a vision of a small, fair-haired girl,' smiled Basil.

His bold eyes, fixed on Stella, said distinctly: 'But you are very much more beautiful, and I admire you. . . .'

Stella said nothing. Julian gave a short laugh.

'Well, you were wrong, my dear chap.'

'I don't blame Basil for what he thought,' put in Lady Eden from her arm-chair. 'I was very taken aback when I first saw darling Pamela. I think her name is deceptive. It doesn't suit her one bit. It is too – too frivolous. She has the type of face that deserves a more noble name.'

Still Stella remained silent – her face retaining its painful flush. If Lady Eden knew the truth . . . she would despise her . . . she would not think her worthy of anything noble. And she thought of the real Pamela – the golden-haired, blue-eyed girl of Basil's imagination. He was not far wrong!

'Pamela dear,' said Lady Eden, 'perhaps you wouldn't mind going to see Hannah and making arrangements about the bedrooms for to-night.'

Glad to escape, Stella rose.

'Yes, dear, I'll see to things,' she said.

The two men rose as she passed from the drawing-room. She looked at neither of them. With downcast head she hurried out to the hall. Her thoughts were chaotic.

What could she do about the rooms? She was helpless. There was no other spare room to which she or Julian could adjourn. This visit from Basil Hargreaves had forced them into very serious difficulties.

She would have to dicuss things with Julian, as soon as she saw him alone. At the moment she could do nothing but carry out Lady Eden's wishes, and give Hannah the order to prepare the room.

Later that day, just before the evening meal, the opportunity to see Julian alone, presented itself. Basil was talking to his aunt in the drawing-room, and Julian had strolled out on the lawn.

Stella walked towards him. The beauty of the sunset sky, crimson, gold, violet, behind the shadow of the distant forest, seemed to hurt her physically as she gazed at it. The lovely serenity mocked the ghastly state of her mind.

Julian was standing rigid, a cigarette between his lips, his dark brows contracted. Obviously his own thoughts were none too pleasant or placid. Stella looked at him, then looked back at the sunset. Everything seemed blacker and more hopeless, this evening. Perhaps it was because she knew that she loved Julian; that ever since Henry Waldon had gone away, she had been aching for one kind word from the man with whom she was playing such a devastating part.

'Julian,' she said in a low voice.

He turned to her, removing his cigarette from his mouth with habitual courtesy.

'You want me?'

'Yes. I – must speak to you. About this – this room . . . What can we do?'

He avoided meeting her eyes, but was conscious of her embarrassment. He stared moodily at the bed of tall pink hollyhocks in front of him.

'I don't know,' he said. 'It is a beastly nuisance. I could murder my cousin for coming just at this juncture of affairs. However, whatever happens we mustn't let mother guess.'

'I know that,' said Stella impatiently.

'We'll manage somehow,' he muttered.

'But how? Don't you realise how awkward it is?'

'Good lord! Of course I do,' he broke out moving his handsome head with a gesture of intense irritation. 'I tell you, we'll manage. You are, I see, dressed for dinner. I'll go up and dress now.'

Stella gave a nervous little laugh, and swallowed hard.

'Yes – but later, it is later that worries me.'

'We will have to go up together – as though nothing were wrong,' said Julian, flinging his cigarette away and pulling another from his case. 'Then, when everyone is asleep, I'll clear out – sleep on the drawing-room sofa.'

'But supposing the maids find you there?'

'They won't. I shan't oversleep. I don't get much sleep nowadays,' he said. 'Since my crash, I've not been able to – thanks to my rotten nerves.'

'I'm sorry,' said Stella gently.

'Spare your pity,' he said, rather brutally. 'And don't get panic-stricken about to-night. I'll see to things. It will only be for a couple of nights, I hope. If Basil doesn't go home Monday, I'll give him a broad hint that he is not wanted.'

'I don't like him,' said Stella.

'I've never been very keen on him, but mother seems to like him. He is a young rotter, too, but old ladies seem to find these rotters attractive. They are very plausible. If mother knew the sort of life Basil leads, she'd loathe him, too. However, he can't do much harm down here, although I daresay he'll try to flirt with you. He flirts with every woman he meets – married or single.'

'He won't get any encouragement,' said Stella with heightened colour.

'Just as well,' said Julian sardonically.

She turned and walked away from him into the drawing-room.

'How he hates me,' she thought wearily.

Through the open French windows, Basil Hargreaves

saw her coming. He had seen her speaking to Julian, and being a very observant person, had noticed the brevity of the conversation and the peculiar expression on both their faces.

'Something is wrong,' Basil mentally decided. 'I wonder what it is. I must watch. . . .'

He looked eagerly at Stella as she entered the drawing-room. She was exquisite in that black chiffon gown, with the jet-straps banding the creamy-whiteness of her smooth shoulder . . . exquisite, cold and aloof. She roused swift passion in the man who since he had left college, had steeped himself in wild love-affairs with one woman after another. He was not happy, unless acting the rôle of lover to some girl.

He told himself to-night, that he would like to be the lover of 'Pamela' . . . Her very coolness attracted him. He was tired of too-ready response. He was entirely without scruples, and the knowledge that this girl was Julian's wife did not lessen his desire to make love to her. He was the type to whom forbidden fruit is the most desirable.

Stella sat down by Lady Eden, and picked up an illustrated paper.

'Oh, don't read – come and talk to me, cousin Pamela,' murmured Basil.

She looked at the slim figure in the immaculate dinner-jacket; at the sleek, fair hair; the weak, dissolute young face of Julian's cousin. She read what was written in his eyes, and despised him for it. But she was forced to be polite.

'What shall we talk about?' she said.

'Do you dance?' he said.

'No – not much.'

'Well, I'm crazy about it,' he said. 'Look here, there's a gramophone in the corner. Let's put on a record and dance.'

'I'd rather not,' said Stella stiffly.

Basil bit his lip.

'Little icicle,' he thought. 'I'd like to kiss those red lips of yours until you thawed to me . . . .' Aloud he said, 'Oh, do come and dance.'

'Yes, do, dear,' put in Lady Eden. 'I'd love to see you young people dancing.'

Stella glanced at Lady Eden's sweet, frail face, and her lips trembled slightly. Dear, innocent old lady! What a great deal Stella would have given for the happy ignorance in which Julian's mother existed.

'Well, let's wait until Julian comes down,' she said at length.

'Darling Pamela just won't do anything without Julian,' said Lady Eden, with a soft laugh. 'They're a ridiculously devoted couple, Basil.'

'H'm,' said Basil.

Stella, swiftly glancing at him, wondered what he meant by the non-committal reply.

CHAPTER 7

About half-past eleven that same night, Stella and Julian sat in the big softly-lighted bedroom which Hannah had prepared for them – the girl on the edge of the bed, still in her black evening gown; the man in a chair by the window.

Stella looked white and tired. Julian's face wore a curious, strained look, and he smoked incessantly. Absolute silence reigned in the house. Now and then a breeze made the curtains bulge a little and flap back against the window; now and then from the garden came the mournful screech of an owl.

Stella sat with her ams locked loosely in her lap, her dark head bowed. She was deep in thought – not happy or peaceful thought. A veritable storm of emotion was making her heart throb and ache. She dared not raise her eyes and look at Julian's rigid figure by the window. It seemed so strange, so unreal that this man, whom she loved unrightfully, should be sitting here in this bedroom with her, so late at night, preserving an attitude of frigid conventionality – waiting his opportunity to slip downstairs.

Again an owl's hoot broke the silence of the summer night.

Stella started and looked up. She shivered a little.

'I do hate that sound,' she whispered. 'It's so depressing.'

Julian pitched his cigarette out of the window and stood up, hands in his pockets, his brows drawn together in that rather sullen frown with which Stella was now familiar.

'This is getting on my nerves,' he muttered. 'We've been sitting here for over an hour.'

'I'm sure everbody is asleep,' said Stella.

'There'd be the deuce to pay if anyone saw me leave this room, fully dressed, and remain downstairs. . . .'

'Take off your coat and put on your dressing-gown,' suggested Stella.

He slipped out of his dinner-jacket and put on the thin silk Chinese dressing-gown which Hannah had carefully laid out on the bed beside Stella's satin wrapper. Stella watched him tie the cord about his waist. With a tired little thrill at her heart she thought how extraordinarily intimate this seemed; how amazing that such a situation should ever have evolved from her desire to make Lady Eden happy.

Julian extracted his cigarette-case from his dinner-jacket.

'I mustn't smoke any more in this room,' he muttered. 'I've made it thick with smoke already.'

'I don't mind,' said Stella, 'only it isn't good for you to smoke so much.'

For a moment his blue, cynical eyes rested on her. Through the thin haze of smoke, her face appeared delicately lovely and very tired.

His heart missed a beat – raced savagely on.

If this girl had been his wife! If only the past could be wiped out; if only he could wake from this nightmare to discover that Stella Morris had always belonged to him. . . that his marriage to Pamela had never taken place. . . .

But the next instant he was inwardly jeering at his own sentiments.

'Stella Morris is a fraud – an impersonator – undeserving of love and tenderness,' he told himself.

'I'm going downstairs now,' he said aloud.

Stella rose.

'I think it is safe,' she said in a low tone. 'I – I'm sorry you have had to – to spend such a trying hour. Good-night.'

He came up to her and gripped both her arms, looking darkly down into her eyes.

'I don't know why I am such a fool as to consider your feelings and act the perfect gentleman with you,' he said brusquely. 'You are being treated much too leniently. Do you know that?'

Immovable in his hold she looked back at him, her emotions under rigid control.

'Do you think I am getting off scot-free?' she asked in a bitter voice. 'Do you think the whole business is not tearing my nerves to pieces – as well as yours?'

'No doubt.'

'Then why regret your – leniency?'

'I merely wonder why I have not made you pay the full price for your impersonation of – my wife,' he said.

She clenched her hands, and a wave of scarlet dyed her face and beautiful throat. She bit her lower lip to keep herself from crying out aloud. Julian's brutalities hurt so much more than he knew . . . it was as though he trampled on her with heavy, nailed boots.

'Julian, isn't it rather late at night to start recriminations and nourish your desire for revenge?' she asked.

He shrugged his shoulders. Bending his head, he kissed her on the mouth – a slow, deliberate kiss that was a long-drawn out agony to the woman who loved him and who knew that kiss to be an insult.

'Good night,' he said, releasing her.

He turned and opened the door. He looked into the dark passage, then walked out and shut the door soundlessly behind him.

Once he was gone, Stella's control vanished, her bitterness of pain and misery broke through the fine reserve which she maintained in his presence. She flung herself face downwards on the bed and buried her face in the pillow. Her tears soaked the cool linen case; her body shook with great, aching sobs. She felt broken and hopeless – more hopeless to-night than she had felt since this thing had begun. If she could have hated Julian Eden, she could have played her part so much more easily – because she would have been callous. She could have met hate with hate . . . laughed him to scorn.

But she loved him, as only a woman of her strong temperament can love. To feel his hand upon her; his lips on her mouth, spelt unending anguish. Intensely proud, she could not have borne that he should guess her state of mind. That would have been the last straw. For, of course, he would despise her the more.

She felt this night that she was going down into the very depths of despair – down – down –down.

Midnight had passed when at last, sick and blind with crying, she dragged herself from her bed and stumbled to the mantelpiece whereon Julian's photograph stood beside that of Pamela.

Her poor blurred eyes turned from Julian's face to the pretty, care-free one of her sister. A short sharp sigh escaped her.

'Oh, Pam, Pam, what a terrible lot of suffering you have to account for,' she whispered. 'Julian's – mine – Geoffrey's — and perhaps, one day— your own!'

When morning came, Julian—after a broken sleep on the drawing-room sofa—managed to get upstairs again and into his bathroom before the servants were about. Thus, by the time the maid awakened Stella with early morning tea, Julian was dressed and out on his hunter for an early-morning run. He felt he needed the fresh air to blow away the cobwebs of the night.

So far as he knew, he had successfully prevented suspicion from arising in the minds of anyone in the house. The process would have to be repeated to-night, of course. And on the morrow Basil Hargreaves must go.

At breakfast-time, Basil was the only one to appear fresh and smiling and in good spirits.

Julian was flushed from the exertion of riding, but silent

and moody. Stella— in spite of having rubbed her cheeks with a rough towel—looked haggard and white.

Basil watched the couple closely, without appearing to do so. Last night, unknown to them, he had sat up till the small hours of the morning, smoking and drinking. That was his latest vice. He liked to sit alone and 'soak' whisky until sleep overpowered him. A disgusting habit, and it was no small wonder that he looked as well as he did. Last night, as he had sat in his bedroom, pouring out one drink after another, he had heard Julian and 'his wife' talking. They had talked quietly, but the walls of Eden Hall were not very thick, and although no words were distinguishable, the murmur of voices was plain.

Interested, Basil had turned out his light, opened his bedroom door the fraction of an inch, and listened.

Then he had heard Julian say: '*I wonder why I have not made you pay the full price for your impersonation of my wife. . . .*'

That had been sufficient to set Basil agog with curiosity and excitement. 'Impersonation . . . ' What had that meant? The word stimulated him far more than the whisky. He put the latter away and strained his ears to hear more. Stella's reply had been inaudible. But he had heard Julian say 'Good night' very abruptly; and later, seen him creep out of the room and go downstairs.

After that had come the sound of muffled weeping from the room next door—a sound that still further intrigued Basil Hargreaves.

For the next hour he had sat up thinking, puzzling—piecing things together.

It was all so amazing and perplexing, that he could not come to any definite conclusion, nor pretend to understand the situation. But he did realise that this dark-haired, grey-eyed girl was *not* Mrs. Julian Eden. She was impersonating Julian's wife. They apparently desired to keep up the deception; but they did not live together. Julian left her room as soon as he believed the rest of the household to be asleep.

This morning Basil looked slyly from his cousin to Stella, and smiled. It was obvious to him now that these two were not married and not in love. Something very funny was 'up.' Well, it would make this an extraordinarily interesting week-end. He would soon find out the truth. Not through old Julian . . . but through the girl. She appealed very strongly to Basil. Now that he knew she was, for some unknown reason, impersonating Julian's wife, he would make use of that knowledge.

Stella, who was making a poor attempt to eat breakfast, looked up and caught Basil's eye. He smiled at her. It was a queer, knowing smile that made her heart leap in a frightened way.

'Going to play tennis with me this morning cousin Pamela?' he asked easily.

Stella breathed again.

'I daresay,' she said. 'I don't know what Julian is going to do.'

'You two play tennis by all means,' said Julian. 'I'm going into Southampton in the car to do some shopping.'

'Right you are, old chap,' said Basil, humming under his breath.

Stella had no desire whatever to play tennis with Basil. Somehow he repelled her. But she told herself that her nerves were all to pieces and that probably he was quite harmless. Just a foolish, dissipated boy. At any rate she could not refuse to play with him without being downright rude.

Later in the morning she donned a white piqué tennis-frock, got her racquet and strolled down to the sunlit court where Basil, in spotless flannels, his sleek fair head shining, was already knocking a few balls into the net.

Lack of sleep and food had made Stella feel weak and

depressed. She had just seen Julian off in his car. Lady Eden had waved and smiled from her bedroom window, so Julian had put an arm round Stella and kissed her good-bye.

But the arm and the kiss had been icy, and without a word to her he had driven away. That had added to her depression.

She endeavoured to smile at Basil.

'Here I am,' she said. 'Now you'll beat me love set.'

He came up to her. His eyes narrowed as they rested on the pale, lovely face; the graceful figure in the white gown.

'Look here, my dear,' he said. 'I want to talk to you before we begin to play.'

She stared at him surprised and inclined to be offended by his familiar manner.

'To talk to me? What about?'

'I won't beat about the bush,' he said. 'I'll tell you right away. *I know.*'

The blood rushed to her cheeks, and receded again, leaving her very white. She put a hand to her heart, because it beat so violently.

'You know—what?'

'That you are not my cousin Julian's wife.'

Completely taken aback she stared at him speechless. She felt cold with dismay as she realised the full significance of his words. *He knew . . . that she was not Julian's wife.*

Had she been less dismayed, less astonished, she might have laughed and jeered at Basil's remark. But she was already too overwrought and desperate to take full command of this critical situation. And her silence gave Basil additional strength.

'Yes. I daresay you are surprised that I should know,' he added. 'Look here, come and sit down and talk to me.'

He took her arm and led her toward a seat beneath a great chestnut-tree just beyond the tennis-court. She went with him mechanically. She sat down gladly, because she felt her knees shaking beneath her.

'Well,' said Basil softly, 'are you going to explain everything to me, cousin Pamela? I suppose your name *is* Pamela?'

Stella found speech at last.

'What do you mean?' she asked hoarsely. 'How have you – made this discovery?'

'I heard what Julian said to you, last night. I saw him leave your room.'

'That does not prove that I am not – his wife,' said Stella desperately..

'Oh, yes it does. He called you his wife's impersonator! That speaks for itself.'

'Oh, my God,' thought Stella. 'Why did Julian not guess that Basil might be eavesdropping!'

She buried her face in her hands a moment – striving for composure – wondering what to say to this man. She felt him touch her shoulder, and looked up again.

'Well,' she asked dully. 'What do you want?'

'An explanation,' he said.

'You had better ask – Julian.'

'I prefer to ask you,' he said.

'I shall not tell you without Julian's permission.'

'Come, that's stupid,' said Basil. 'You must tell me.'

'Must!' she repeated the word resentfully.

'Unless you want me to ask Aunt Cecily.'

He saw the look of fear that leaped into her eyes.

'No – no – good heavens! no, you must not breathe a word to her of what you have heard,' she said.

'She does not know, then?'

'No – of course not.'

'Ah,' said Basil, raising his brows reflectively. 'I see. Aunt Cecily is delicate – has heart-trouble. Of course, I see – She must be spared any worry.'

'Yes.'

'Then you might as well tell me your story,' Basil said, in his persuasive voice. 'Come along.'

Stella made a gesture of infinite weariness.

'Oh, well, since you know so much – why not everything? But you must swear before God that you will not let Lady Eden guess.'

'I shall not tell her,' he said.

And for the next few minutes he sat silent, his curious, interested gaze resting on the girl, while she unfolded the story of her impersonation of Pamela.

When she had finished, he drew a deep breath.

'By Jove! You're a sport,' he said admiringly.

Stella frowned.

'And old Julian is a fool,' he added. 'A fool not to – you beautiful thing!'

'Oh, how dare you?' Stella said in a low, quivering voice. 'How dare you?'

His hand stole out and gripped her bare arm.

'I've fallen in love with you,' he whispered. 'I've been in love with you for the last twenty-four hours. Now that I know you are not Julian's wife, there is no reason why I should not – tell you of my love.'

She wrenched her arm away, her eyes blazing, her breast heaving.

'There is every reason,' she said. 'You are base and vile to speak to me in this way. When Julian knows. . . .'

'He will not know,' broke in Basil. 'You are not going to tell him that I know the truth, my dear *Stella*.'

She flushed, but held her head proudly.

'He shall know – as soon as he returns.'

'I say he shall not,' said Basil, very quietly. He caught one of the girl's hands in his again. Passion flamed in his eyes now, and his breath quickened. 'You and I are going to understand each other, my dear. If you tell Julian that I know the truth, I shall go straight to Aunt Cecily with your pretty little tale of deception.'

Aghast, she stared at him.

'You would do that? Oh, you *couldn't!*'

'I could do anything for the sake of winning one kind

word from your lovely lips,' he said in a low voice. 'Be kind to me Stella, and Aunt Cecily shall not know.'

'You cad!' she flung at him. 'Julian shall be told and he will turn you out of Eden Hall.'

'Very well. And before I go, Aunt Cecily shall learn why I am going.'

Stella put a hand up to her throbbing temples.

'Good heavens, what are you driving at? What are you threatening me like this for?' she demanded.

'I merely state that I will keep your secret and spare Aunt Cecily, so long as you are kind to me,' he said. 'Need I explain more fully?'

'Yes – I think it is necessary for you to explain – much more fully,' said Stella, in answer to Basil's question.

He shrugged his shoulders.

'My dear girl, you aren't so blind and innocent as all that,' he said. 'You must see that I—am in love with you.

Stella stared at him. Then she gave a scornful laugh.

'In love with me . . . when you have only just met me! How absurd! You must be joking.'

'No. I am deadly earnest,' he said. 'I have never been more serious. I am in love with you, Stella, and I want you to return my love.'

'But how can I? Are you mad? And what has all this got to do with – the secret you have unearthed?'

'I'd better tell you outright,' he said. 'If you accept me as – a lover, I will keep your secret and see that Aunt Cecily does not guess. I will also see that Julian does not guess that I know.'

A long silence followed his speech. Stella's heart beat furiously. She felt hot, sick with shame; with impotent rage against this cad who dared threaten her – dared make such outrageous suggestions.

He had discovered that she was not Julian's wife, and he was going to blackmail her – not for money – but for love; at least it was passion – the name 'love' ought not to be so desecrated. She shivered and turned her face from him in loathing.

'I understand what you mean,' she said. 'But I don't understand how you can be so utterly vile.'

' "All's fair in love and war," ' he quoted. 'I am a funny chap – and when I want a thing I do anything to get it. I want you. I can't have you yet – until this tangle with Julian has been unravelled; and that won't be, presumably, until Aunt Cecily dies. But I can at least love you – hold you in my arms now and then – steal a kiss when the occasion presents itself. . . .'

She turned her head and looked at him again; saw the burning desire in his eyes. The man was in deadly earnest.

Almost Stella hated herself for having aroused such passion in Julian's cousin; hated the physical beauty that could turn a civilised well-bred man into an unscrupulous cad.

'Listen, Stella,' continued Basil. 'If you tell Julian that I know the truth and that I have asked for your love, I shall go straight to Aunt Cecily. I warn you. . . .'

'You would have the death of an innocent old lady on your soul?'

He had the grace to flush, but immediately laughed.

'It wouldn't be my fault if she succumbed to a heart-attack. The fault would be yours, for deceiving her.'

'Basil,' said Stella, in a voice of despair. 'Won't you be fair and decent about things, and – and keep silent just for your aunt's sake?'

He gripped her wrist and held it between thin, flexible fingers. She shivered again as she looked down and saw them. They were peculiarly cruel, grasping sort of hands. He was good-looking, this fair-haired, blue-eyed young man – yet utterly vicious and repellent – a very different stamp of man to his cousin, Julian Eden.

'I want you to be kind to me, Stella,' he repeated. 'If you will – then I will keep silence.'

'What must you think I'm made of?' she asked in a passionate undertone. 'Do you think that I can go on acting my part as Julian's wife, and allow familiarities from you into the bargain?'

'It won't be for long,' he said. 'Only while I'm here.'

'You must go tomorrow,' she said, her breast heaving, her cheeks fiery-red. 'You can see how difficult you are making things – the bedroom – the – '

'Oh, yes, I'll leave Eden Hall to-morrow,' he broke in. 'I don't want you to be forced into sharing a room with Julian. I'm much too much in love with you to risk Julian's falling in love.'

Stella's heart have an agonising jerk.

'He is not likely to do that,' she said.

'Do you want him to?'

'What right have you to question me?'

'I am answered,' said Basil, smiling. 'I suppose you are foolish enough to be in love with your temporary husband. Oh, well! That must cease. I want you, Stella – want you more than I've ever wanted any other woman. I suppose it's your infernal coldness, as well as your beauty – ' He drew nearer to her. 'Iceberg,' he whispered. 'I'd give my soul to thaw you – to make you respond to my passion.'

'I shall never do that,' she said shrinking back. 'Please let go of my wrist.'

'No. And you must understand that I claim the right to make love to you – when I can,' he said calmly. 'I shall leave Eden Hall in the morning, and put up at the 'Crown,' in Lyndhurst, so that I can be near you. You will have to see me in the forest sometimes, and I will come here at times, presumably to see Aunt Cecily. Nobody will be the wiser. My mother has suggested that I should remain in the forest until my health improves. Too many late nights in town have knocked me up!'

Stella began to tremble. She felt utterly tired of fighting – striving in vain to do the right thing.

'Oh, leave me alone,' she said piteously. 'Don't add to my burden – it is heavy enough, God knows.'

'Try and care for me, Stella,' he whispered. 'Let my love bring you happiness.'

'It is not love,' she said hotly. 'If you loved me you would not threaten to bully me.'

He moved his head impatiently.

'I won't argue the point. Only understand, my dear, that one word to Julian and – Aunt Cecily knows the truth. . . .'

Stella buried her face in her hands. A long bitter sigh broke from her lips. She was faced with another mighty problem. Either she must conform to Basil's horrible plans or – risk his opening Lady Eden's eyes. Were the latter to happen, all hers and Julian's efforts to make the old lady's last hours happy would have been in vain. Besides, if she died suddenly and unhappily, Julian would never get over it. His love for his mother was all-absorbing. He would blame her, Stella. He would think she ought to have made any sacrifice rather than allow the catastrophe to occur.

It meant fresh torture for her; the torture of remaining passive, unable to object, when this dissolute young man chose to make love to her.

'Well?' came Basil's drawling voice. 'Have you decided?'

She raised her head – looked at him with tragic grey eyes.

'I can't let Lady Eden suffer,' she said. 'I will do – anything within reason that you ask of me.'

'Sensible girl!' he said triumphantly.

And the next moment she felt his hands about her waist - and his lips touch her mouth.

The contact seemed to change her from a passive martyr into a flashing torch of resentment. She sprang to her feet, eyes blazing, cheeks peony-red.

'Oh – it is intolerable. I can't – I won't bear it!' she gasped.

Basil laughed lightly and stood up beside her.

'That was a very brief kiss, my dear,' he said. 'The next

one must be – longer. And now, hadn't we better play our game of tennis? Aunt Cecily might take it into her head to stroll down here and watch us.'

Stella stood mute a moment, striving desperately for self-control. At length the colour receded from her face, leaving it white and tired. She drew a long breath of resignation and picked up her racquet.

'I'm afraid I shall not be able to play,' she said. 'I don't feel up to it. I shall tell Lady Eden that I am – feeling the heat.'

'Oh, very well,' said Basil. 'Just as you like. But remember, Stella – not a word – to Julian – or I will not answer for consequences.'

'I quite understand that,' she said. 'And will you please remember that I am known here as *Pamela*. It is extremely dangerous for you to make use of my real name.'

'Little Cousin Pam!' he mocked. 'What a joke! By Jove, the whole affair is amazing. I'd never have dreamed of such bribery and corruption in the serene Eden household. The family has always looked upon Aunt Cecily's branch as the peaceful, prim and proper one.'

'Lady Eden is a saint,' said Stella. 'And Julian is good – a good man. You have no right to suggest otherwise. The affair is my fault. I had no right to come here and pose as Julian's widow. But I did it for Lady Eden's sake . . . she seemed so lonely, so longing for a daughter's companionship and comfort.'

Basil came up to her and put his hands on her shoulders. He bent and kissed her on both cheeks in a light, yet possessive fashion that made her thrill with anger.

'Don't trouble to excuse yourself, my fairest flower,' he whispered. 'I consider you have been sporting and admirable all the way through. I don't know what the real Pamela is like, but I'm sure she can't be half as charming as yourself.'

With a gesture of exasperation the girl turned from him

and walked swiftly across the tennis-court, toward the house. Basil dropped back on the bench under the chestnut-tree. He drew a cigarette from his case, tapped it with a slow, deliberate movement, then looked at Stella's slim figure, quickly disappearing from view.

His eyes narrowed. He smiled and began to hum beneath his breath, while he smoked.

CHAPTER 8

Stella paused beside Lady Eden, who sat as usual in her invalid's chair just outside the dining-room windows; a purple silk parasol protecting her from the hot rays of the sun.

'How are you, Mother dear?' Stella asked gently.

Lady Eden looked up from her daily paper and stretched out a thin, frail hand to the girl.

'Very well, thank you, Pamela darling. I seem to have grown stronger and happier every day since my boy – I mean *our* boy – returned.'

Stella winced. 'Our boy!' If only Lady Eden knew how little Julian belonged to her, Stella! . . . But she took the frail hand and pressed it tightly to hers.

'I am so glad, dear,' she said. 'It is wonderful for Julian and me to see you improve in health like this.'

'The Age of Miracles has not passed after all,' murmured Lady Eden. 'When I first came to London to see you, my dear, I felt myself to be very near the end. I felt that I was drifting slowly into the shadows . . . broken-hearted . . . hopeless . . . my husband and son both gone . . . and nobody left to me. But your coming made all the difference in the world. And Julian's return has completed the miracle for me.'

Stella bit her lip. She felt the tears starting to her eyes. She suddenly knelt down beside the old lady, who immediately put her arm around her.

With her dark head in the circle of that loving arm, Stella

rested a moment in comparative happiness and peace. All the sin, the sorrow, the folly of her impersonation; the wicked cunning of Basil Hargreaves, were forgotten. She was just a tired child who crept into its mother's arms for rest.

'My dear,' said Lady Eden, looking down at her. 'You are crying. Why? Child, how emotional you are! Does the thought of Julian's return still move you to tears?'

'Yes – perhaps it does,' said Stella huskily. 'And still more so, the thought that I have contributed a little toward making you well and happy again, Mother dear.'

Lady Eden smiled, and patted the girl's cheek.

'You are a sweet, kind-hearted child, Pamela,' she said. 'Julian is lucky to have won your love.'

Stella closed her eyes tightly, but the burning tears forced their way beneath the sealed lids and coursed down her cheeks. She had to bite her lower lip fiercely in order to keep herself from sobbing aloud . . . from throwing herself on the mercy of Julian's mother . . . telling her the truth.

But it was impossible. All the sacrifices she had made, and must go on making, were for the sake of keeping the truth from Lady Eden. Julian idolised her; she, Stella, loved her sincerely. Neither of them could bear the thought of losing her. Yet, what was to be done should she live on for many years? It would be useless to try to keep up this farce for any length of time.

'And it is useless to try to think for one day ahead,' Stella told herself wretchedly. 'It is a question of waiting . . . waiting until the tangle unravels itself.'

She wiped away her tears and made an effort to smile. Then she kissed Julian's mother and rose to her feet.

'I found the sun too hot down on the court, Mother,' she observed. 'I am going to sit indoors awhile.'

'That's right, darling,' said Lady Eden. 'Take care of yourself, or Julian will be after you.'

Stella's lips twisted into a bitter smile as she walked into the house.

She had no desire to take care of herself, and Julian would not mind what happened to her. He did not care. . . .

All that was bad enough. The shadow of Basil's passion, his desire for secret meetings, made things a thousand times worse. How would it all end? She dared not think.

Just before lunch-time, Julian returned from Southampton. Stella was in her bedroom, a silk dressing-jacket over her frock. She had been lying on her bed for the last hour, with the blinds down and a handkerchief soaked in eau-de-Cologne on her forehead, hoping that the rest and quiet might soothe her jangled nerves.

The door opened and Julian walked in. He paused as he saw the girl.

'Oh, I beg your pardon,' he said awkwardly. 'I didn't think you would be here.'

'Please don't mind,' said Stella, trying to speak in a normal voice, but her face flooded with colour as she realised that her hair was down her back. She began hastily to pin it up.

Julian stood hesitating a moment. He had never seen Stella's hair down before. It was a wonderful mass – dark, glossy waves of it nearly reaching her knees.

He felt strangely tongue-tied as he watched her coil it with slim, deft fingers about her head. Deep down in him had crept a queer longing to plunge his hands into that dusky cloud of hair – to wind it about his throat. He had always loved women's hair – beautiful hair, like Stella's.

The coiffure completed, Stella slipped off her dressing-jacket and faced Julian. She felt less embarrassed now. She gave him a swift, shy glance. He looked tired, as though the motor-ride into Southampton had done him no good. Of course, she must remember he was not very strong, after that crash. . . .

'I hope you had a successful morning's shopping,' she said politely.

'Thanks,' he said. 'I bought some collars and ties, and two or three odd things I needed. I also found rather a nice book for my mother . . . ' He drew a parcel from under his arm and handed it to Stella. 'It's a copy of 'Virginibus Puerisque,' he added. 'She is very fond of it, and told me last night she had lent somebody her edition, some months ago, and lost it.'

Stella looked at the little red, morocco-bound book, nodded and handed it back to Julian.

'Yes, it a beautiful edition. It will delight mother,' she said.

The conversation between them was entirely natural, if a little stilted, They might indeed have been husband and wife. And there had been something unusually friendly in the way Julian had handed the book to her, Stella reflected. Was he feeling in a more friendly mood? Did he hate her a little less?

His next words brought more balm to her sore, aching heart.

'You are looking very washed-out,' he said. 'I hope you are not feeling ill.'

The solicitude for her health touched her deeply. She swallowed hard before she answered.

'Thank you – I am quite well. I daresay all the – the worry of the last week or two has upset me a little.'

'I'm sorry,' said Julian. He cleared his throat and his forehead contracted. 'Of course, the whole business is upsetting to both of us. I'm not feeling particularly well myself. I daresay Pamela is the happiest of us all. She would be!' he added with a sardonic laugh.

Stella locked her hands together.

'Oh, she can't be happy in her heart,' she said. 'She must feel awful at times, knowing that she is not poor Geoffrey's real wife.'

'Some women have no conscience,' said Julian. 'And my charming wife, Pamela, is one of that kind, I think.'

Then he added, with a queer, brief glance at Stella:

'But you – well, I believe you have a conscience. I imagine so.'

'In that case you can be certain that I am being amply punished for my wrong-doing,' said Stella.

Julian pulled out a cigarette and lit it. It is the man's way of hiding his feelings. And at the moment he had felt the first, faint desire to be very kind and gentle to this girl – to bury his prejudices – his desire to 'make her pay.'

'Did you and Basil play tennis?' he asked, abruptly changing the conversation.

'No. I did not feel up to it,' she added.

The name of Basil made her feel suddenly cold and troubled. Basil had not finished with her. Of that she was sure. If only she dared tell Julian that Basil *knew* . . . of his threats . . . but she could not. The thought of the frail, sweet, innocent old lady downstairs sealed her lips.

'There goes the gong,' said Julian. 'Lunch is ready.'

In silence they walked downstairs.

The rest of the day passed so naturally and peacefully that Stella felt sure it must end with a catastrophe. Such peace was too good to last. Basil was at his best; he played two sets of tennis with Julian after lunch, and read to his aunt, after tea . . . the model nephew! Julian was in a softened mood and treated Stella with a kindness that was as sweet as it was unexpected.

During tea, there occurred one little incident which stood out in her mind long afterwards. She had taken the handle of the big family silver teapot and found it too hot. Her exclamation of pain had brought Julian to her side at once.

'I say, take my handkerchief, darling,' he had said.

Stella had looked swiftly round the room. Lady Eden was smiling; Basil was looking at her with an amused expression in his eyes. She had tilted her head almost defiantly and looked back at Julian.

'Thank you, darling,' she had answered.

Their hands had touched as he transferred the handkerchief into her fingers. Their eyes had met. And he had smiled – not forcedly – but spontaneously, as though a sudden stream of sympathy flowed between them.

Her heart had given a great leap – raced wildly on. She had continued pouring out the tea, her cheeks flushed, long lashes hiding the light in her eyes.

And she had thought:

'He does not hate me so much . . . it was a real smile – he gave me a real smile. . . .'

It had made her pathetically happy for the rest of that day.

Yet she had had the premonition that this was only a lull in the storm. And she was right. The storm broke out again with renewed fury, that same night.

Lady Eden retired to bed at her usual early hour. Julian helped her upstairs, with Hannah on the other side. Stella found herself alone in the drawing-room with Basil. She had dreaded being left alone with him, and gave him a nervous look after the door had closed.

He did not look at her for a moment, but sauntered to the gramophone and wound it up, then put on a record.

'Two years old, that one-step,' he remarked. 'You must get something new in the way of dancing music, Pamela.'

'I don't dance much,' she said coldly.

'Well, come and dance with me now,' he said, smiling and holding out his arms.

'No, thank you.'

'Come and dance,' repeated Basil an imperious note in his voice.

Stella hesitated. Then her cheeks hot with resentment, she unwillingly rose.

'I don't see why I should,' she said.

'But you will,' he murmured. 'You will do anything – almost *anything* that I ask, my dearest dear.'

His familiarity sickened her. She shivered as he put an arm around her and forced her to dance.

'I like you in that pearl-grey chiffon gown,' he whispered in her ear. 'You are like Psyche rising from the grey mist of the sea.'

'You are very poetic,' Stella said, unable to refrain from sneering.

His mood changed with lightning-like rapidity. His blue eyes narrowed. She felt his arm pressing her waist like steel.

'Be kind to me – be nice to me,' he said. 'If you sneer at my pretty speeches, you will make me angry.'

'I prefer your anger to your pretty speeches,' she said shortly.

'Or this? . . . .'

He paused in the dance, swung her head down on to his shoulder and kissed her – a passionate, savage kiss that made her blanch and clench her hands.

He grew drunk with her beauty and her lips – lost his head. Holding her close, he kissed her again and again . . . mouth, cheeks. throat, and cool bare shoulders.

Precisely at that moment, the door opened and Julian walked into the room.

The two men faced each other. There was a long, tense silence. Then Julian walked up to his cousin and struck him across the face.

'You cur!' he said. 'How dare you make love to my wife?'

Basil reeled back, a hand to the cheek that Julian had struck. There was a red mark upon it. He crouched, like an animal that has been hit and is about to spring back. But he changed his mind. He gave a quick, nervous laugh.

'Really, Julian,' he said, 'there is no need to be so violent.'

Julian marched to the door and flung it open.

'Get out,' he said. 'Pack your things and go home. I won't have you in my house another night.'

'Confound it all,' said Basil, 'you needn't treat a fellow like that. Your – wife seemed quite inclined to – like my love making. It was only a bit of sport and –'

'Any more, and I'll get my hunting-crop and thrash you,' broke in Julian in a low, dangerous voice. 'Get out – before I lose my temper altogther.'

Basil straightened his collar, looked at Stella, who was still sitting in the chair with her face hidden, and shrugged his shoulders.

He had been a fool to risk Julian catching him at this game, of course. It was too late to be sorry about that. He would have to go. But it would only be as far as the 'Crown,' Lyndhurst. He was not going to Southampton; to lose all chances of holding Stella in his arms again. The touch of her, the memory of those kisses he had stolen had made him doubly anxious to possess her beauty. And he would not let Julian know that he knew Stella was *not* Mrs. Julian Eden . . . that would be playing into Julian's hands. No! He would keep that as a lever against Stella. He would see more of her – on the 'Q.T.'

He gave a little cough and sauntered to the door.

'Sorry I've – er – annoyed you, Julian,' he said. 'I'd better go. You can tell Aunt Cecily I was called home on business.'

Julian preserved a stony silence. His hands were clenched behind his back. The veins stood out on his forehead like whipcords. He was obviously labouring under violent emotion.

With another swift glance at the girl, Basil walked out of the room.

'Some minutes later there came the sound of his car rolling down the drive away from the house.

At last Stella raised her face. She saw Julian very grim, very white, looking down at her with an expression of contempt in his eyes that made her heart give a sick jerk.

'Well,' he said, 'what have you got to say for yourself?'

'Nothing,' she said dully.

'No – I daresay not . . . ' He laughed. 'You women can be vile, sometimes! I saw you – surrendering to him . . . allowing him to kiss you – my cousin – and you supposed to be my wife! At least, in this house, bearing my name, you might have behaved decently and honourably.'

She flinched under the lash of his words.

'Julian – you don't understand. . . .'

'I understand that you are a despicable flirt,' he interrupted. 'Basil has always been a dissolute wretch, and I warned you against him. But apparently you wanted to flirt with him.'

'No – no!' the cry was wrung from her.

'You can't tell me that,' he said scornfully. 'You were making no attempt to fight him, when I came in.'

Stella felt tortured beyond all endurance. She wanted to cry out: 'It isn't fair – I was forced into it . . . ' to explain to Julian that Basil held their secret – threatened to tell Lady Eden – unless she allowed him to kiss her. And she dared not. Even now, though Basil had gone, she feared him – felt certain he had not gone far and would be ready to pay her out of she told Julian the truth.

'Julian,' she said hoarsely,' 'Please try to believe me when I tell you that I – am not a flirt. I did not want Basil to kiss me.'

'I'm afraid I shall never believe that,' he said. 'But it was only to be expected. A girl who would do what you did in the beginning – would do anything. . . .'

'Oh, don't!' she moaned.

'I shall have no further pity on you,' he continued. 'This morning when I came back from Southampton I felt suddenly sorry for you. I resolved to be kinder and more considerate. Your behaviour with my cousin has altered my attitude entirely. And I tell you this,' he added between his teeth, 'were it not for my mother's sake – were it not necessary for me to continue calling you my wife, I would not let this farce go on one hour longer. I would ask you to accompany Basil – out of this house. Do you hear me?'

'Yes,' she said in a muffled tone. 'I – hear.'

The drawing-room door suddenly opened. Hannah, Lady Eden's maid, hurried in – her face creased with anxiety.

'Oh, Mr. Julian – ma'am,' she gasped. 'Her Ladyship's had another heart-attack, just as I was getting her into bed. I think we ought to have the doctor – at once. She looks very bad, and I'm afraid it's – the end.'

'Another heart-attack!' repeated Julian, his face suddenly paling. 'Phone up for Dr. Bates at once, Hannah. And you, Pamela . . . ' he turned to Stella, everything forgotten except the fact that his idolised mother's life was fast ebbing. 'Come with me to mother. . . .'

'Of course,' breathed the girl.

Hannah rushed into the hall and took up the telephone. Julian ran up the stairs, two at a time, and Stella followed him, her heart throbbing with anxiety. She, too, forgot Basil Hargreaves and the row that had just taken place; all thought was centred upon Lady Eden, for whom she had been making so many sacrifices.

Outside Lady Eden's bedroom door, Julian paused and put his head down to the girl's.

'Very careful', he whispered. 'Careful what you say and do.'

'Of course,' Stella whispered back.

They entered the bedroom together. It was dimly lit by the pink-shaded table lamp beside the bed. Lady Eden lay against her pillows, breathing painfully; her delicate face contracted with the agony of those terrible heart-spasms which attacked her at intervals. She looked so piteously shrunken in the white frilled bed-jacket; eyes closed, lips purplish-blue; nostrils pinched; that it seemed to both

Julian and Stella that the end had indeed come – she could not possibly live.

A small blue bottle, uncorked, was on the table beside her, showing that the resourceful Hannah had already administered a dose of the strong stimulant which Dr. Bates prescribed for these attacks.

There was nothing more to be done now, until the doctor himself appeared.

Julian tiptoed to his mother's side. Stella stood beside him, her throat feeling hot and dry. She realised suddenly how much Julian's mother meant to her; how greatly she had come to love her since she had taken Pamela's place at Eden Hall.

'Mother,' said Julian, bending over the bed, 'Mother darling. . . .'

Lady Eden's eyes slowly opened. Her expression of pain vanished and was replaced by a tender, contented look as she saw her son's handsome face.

'Julian,' she murmured. 'My dear boy. . . .'

Her hand fluttered out to meet his. He knelt down and took the frail fingers in a strong, vital clasp, as though striving to impart some of his own strength into her weak body.

'Mother, how do you feel now?' he asked her.

'Better – darling,' said Lady Eden, very slowly. 'Don't – worry. I shall be – all right – soon. Where is – Pamela?'

'I am here, Mother,' said Stella, coming forward and kneeling beside Julian. 'I am here, dearest.'

Lady Eden smiled at her.

'I feel much better – now that I have seen my two – dear ones,' she whispered. 'So very – dear to me – both of you.'

Her eyelids drooped again, and she lay very still for a few moments, breathing quickly and laboriously.

Julian watched her in an agony of trepidation. He was making a mental calculation of the time Dr. Bates would take to get to Eden Hall. His house was on the outskirts of the village. It would take him ten minutes, at the most, in a car. Heaven grant he came quickly . . . in time to save this precious life.

Lady Eden made no movement for a few moments. Julian retained the nerveless hand in his warm fingers. He glanced at the girl by his side, and was astonished to see her quietly weeping. The tears were rolling down her cheeks – her eyes, fixed on the woman in the bed, were full of sorrow.

Julian's lips twitched. He turned to Stella and stared at his mother again. His thoughts were mixed – perplexed. Stella's whole attitude perplexed him. He believed her to be a heartless flirt – a girl without much decent feeling, after her behaviour with Basil, to-night. Yet she could kneel here and cry – like this – because his mother was dangerously ill; her grief and anxiety were genuine, too – no doubt about that.

His mother loved her . . . he could not forget that . . . could not forget her first cry had been for him – her second for 'Pamela.' My two dear ones . . . 'she called them.

The bitter anger and contempt which he had felt downstairs, some moments ago, faded away. Kneeling there, with Stella at his side, he felt only sick misery – a tremendous sense of desolation. If he lost his mother to-night, he would have nothing left . . . nobody in the world to care for – to care for him.

Stella's tear-blurred eyes left Lady Eden for an instant to look at Julian. She saw his misery, and her heart ached for him. Impulsively she put out a hand and touched his shoulder.

'Julian,' she whispered, 'don't give up hope. You mustn't. . . .'

She half expected him to shrink from her touch and ignore her sympathy. To her surprise he turned to her, as though grateful for her words.

'I'm trying not to,' he whispered back. 'Dr. Bates will be

here any minute now. He is always wonderful with mother.'

They both looked at Lady Eden again; knelt there for some time in silence, keeping anxious vigil. Stella's lips moved in prayer. Her hands were clasped on the bed before her. Some of the anguish that had eaten into her soul, when Julian had hurled his unjust accusations at her, had passed – she felt that Lady Eden's illness had made a bond between them again. Piteously she clutched at that straw of comfort; felt comforted because Julian turned to her in his trouble.

The sound of a car coming up the drive broke the stillness of the summer night. Julian gently released his mother's hand, and stood up.

'That's Bates,' he said in a tone of relief.

Stella also rose and stood there, waiting, while Julian went downstairs to greet the doctor. The two men came up together. Bates was a thin, short man with a clever face and iron-grey hair. He had attended Lady Eden for the last six years, and understood her case thoroughly.

Julian suddenly realised that Bates did not know the girl who stood at the foot of the bed, her dark head inclined, her beautiful face slightly in shadow. He bit his lip and forced himself to make the necessary intoductions.

'Dr. Bates . . . my wife,' he said.

'I am very pleased to meet you, Mrs. Eden,' said Bates shaking hands with her. 'And I must congratulate you on the miraculous return of your husband.'

'Thank you very much,' said Stella.

She was thankful that the doctor then passed on to Lady Eden's bedside. He did not notice her painful flush.

Bates made a swift examination of his patient; laid down his stethoscope, and walked back to Julian and Stella.

'She's pretty feeble, I'm afraid,' he whispered, his face puckered. 'But there's a chance – I don't think the attack is much worse than the one she had last June; and she pulled through that in a marvellous way. She looks very frail, you know, but she has a fine constitution – even now.'

'Thank God for that,' said Julian.

'I'm going to give you another bottle of medicine, to be administered every hour or so, if necessary,' said Bates. 'I shall stay for a few more minutes, then leave her to you.'

'Do you think she wants a nurse?' asked Stella. 'Or could – could I nurse her?'

'I feel sure she will be in capable hands if I leave her with you, Mrs. Eden,' said the doctor. 'There is no real necessity for a trained nurse.'

'Then please let me sit up with her to-night,' said Stella, earnestly. 'I would love to.'

Dr. Bates glanced at Julian.

Julian threw Stella quick look, then stared at the carpet.

'Yes, I don't see why not,' he agreed.

Bates returned to his patient. Lady Eden opened her eyes and greeted the doctor with a smile.

'So sorry – to bring you out – so late,' she whispered.

'Nonsense!' he said cheerily. 'I'm always delighted to see you at any time of the day or night, Lady Eden. You're much better now, though. I'm not going to stay.'

'Of course – not,' she said. 'There is no – need. The pain has – almost gone.'

Bates said a few more words to her, then rejoined the others who had walked to the doorway.

'She'll pull through, I think,' he said. 'Wonderful woman, Lady Eden. But I advise you to watch her, Mrs. Eden, be sure and give her a teaspoonful of this stuff as soon as you see any signs of the pain returning.'

Stella nodded and took the bottle he handed her. He bade her good night and passed downstairs with Julian.

'Very nice to see you again after all this time, my dear fellow,' he said as they went. 'And what a charming woman your wife is.'

'Yes,' said Julian, shortly.

'I don't think I've ever seen a more beautiful face,' continued the doctor. 'Such fine eyes! You're a lucky chap.'

Julian felt the blood rush to his temples. He forced himself to answer in a natural manner. But he was thankful to shut the front door upon Bates. He felt tired out by the emotional events of the evening; his nerves would not stand much chatter about 'his wife.'

He was still too deeply concerned about his mother to think of much else. He deliberately put the memory of his cousin from his mind. He did not want to think of that cad – nor of Stella's extraordinarily lax behaviour.

He met Stella in the corridor outside his mother's bedroom.

'Hadn't you better let Hannah sit up with mother?' he asked brusquely.

'Oh, please trust me to do so!' said Stella, catching her breath. 'I want to – please let me.'

'Oh well, if you want to so much . . . ' he muttered.

'I do,' said Stella. 'Nothing will give me greater pleasure. Whatever I am – whatever you think of me . . . ' her lips quivered . . . . 'I genuinely love your mother.'

Julian dug his hands into his pockets and stared at her, then at the floor.

'Yes, I believe that,' he said.

'Thank you,' she said. 'I am going to slip into my dressing-gown. Then I'll sit in that big arm-chair by mother's bed.'

The queerest feelings attacked Julian as he listened to her. 'Mother's bed. . . .' How naturally she called Lady Eden 'mother'! He did not know whether to feel resentment or pleasure – but he noticed suddenly that the girl's face was terribly white and tired.

'Look here,' he said. 'You can't keep up all night. You look worn out already.'

'I'm quite all right,' she said flushing. 'I'm not a bit tired. . . .'

'You are,' said Julian, gruffly. 'At any rate, Hannah or I can relieve you later on. You'll call me at once, if I'm wanted – won't you?'

'Of course,' she said.

'Good night,' he said awkwardly.

'Good night,' she replied.

He turned, walked into his bedroom and closed the door.

With tears stinging her eyes, Stella sought her room, and prepared for her all-night vigil by Lady Eden's side.

She was tired – deadly tired. Her head ached and throbbed. But she would not give way. Five minutes later she was sitting beside the sick woman, watching every movement with keenest anxiety.

Lady Eden seemed to be asleep. She lay motionless. The house was wrapped in silence, broken occasionally by the mournful hoot of an owl.

Stella's eyes grew heavy with fatigue, and the pain in her temples increased. Now and then she felt her head nodding . . . her eyelids closing. But she pulled herself up with a jerk and rubbed the sleep from her eyes again. She must watch the patient – at any moment Lady Eden might have a fresh spasm of pain and need the medicine.

It was a long, weary vigil. Night-duty is tiring even for trained nurses, who sleep during the day. Stella had had no sleep that day, and thus was doubly fatigued by the effort of sitting up until the small hours of the morning. If Hannah had meant to relieve her, she had apparently overslept, for she did not come.

At three in the morning, when the first faint rays of dawn were creeping through the curtains and filling the room with grey, ghostly light – Stella reached breaking point. The pain in her head had become intolerable, and her eyelids seemed weighted with lead.

The bedroom door opened. Stella's heavy eyes saw, with relief, the tall figure of Julian, in pyjamas and dressing-gown. His hair was ruffled, and he looked as though he had woken up rather suddenly.

'Good Lord! Are you still here?' he asked, advancing toward the girl. 'Hasn't Hannah taken a turn?'

'No,' whispered Stella.

'You must be dead tired,' he said.

'I'm quite all right,' she said.

'Well, I'll look after mother now,' said Julian. 'You go along to your room and get some sleep.'

'She is quite normal and peaceful,' said Stella. 'I haven't had to give her one dose. She has been sleeping.'

'Thank God!' said Julian, with a tender look at his mother.

Stella tried to get out of her chair – and failed. Her limbs seemed cramped. She bit her lip and tried again – gained her feet, but swayed perilously – the pain in her head extending to her whole body. She gave a little muffled cry.

'Oh – I – I'm afraid – I can't walk. . . .'

Julian looked at her swiftly, and his heart suddenly smote him. He saw that she was absolutely exhausted. Her face was white and pinched in the dawn-light, and there were great violent bruises under her eyes.

'My dear girl,' he said, 'you've been overtaxing your strength.'

She gave a feeble smile and tried to walk, but crumpled up at once in a little heap on the carpet. Julian smothered an exclamation. He picked her up in his strong arms and carried her out to the corridor along to her bedroom. She was ridiculously light, he thought – too light. She had not been eating enough – he remembered now, how little she did eat. It struck him as he gazed down at her pale face that she was a mere child. She looked so young with her dark hair in two thick plaits which swung to her hips. Her slim body, in the silk dressing-gown, was soft, pliant against his own.

His former anger against her vanished, leaving only compunction and gratitude because she had kept faithful watch over his mother, and worn herself out.

'My dear,' he said, putting her gently down on her bed, 'you should have sent for me – why didn't you?'

Stella gave a long sigh. She had felt utterly at peace in his strong arms, with her head against his shoulder. If only he could have gone on carrying her – never let her go. . . .

She opened her tired eyes and smiled at him.

'I'm all right. A few hours' sleep will put me right.'

'You mustn't dream of getting up until lunchtime,' he said. 'I'll send Hannah in with your breakfast.'

'Oh, no! . . . ' Stella began.

'Yes,' interrupted Julian masterfully. 'You're fagged out. You must rest.'

Rather awkwardly he picked up a soft satin eiderdown and covered her with it.

'Thank you for staying with mother,' he said.

'Thank *you*,' she whispered. 'Good night, Julian.'

He stood still an instant, staring down at her. He felt suddenly that he wanted to bend down and kiss her – gather her to his heart as he would an erring, repentant child. But he turned and walked out of the room, his brows contracting. He called himself a fool.

She had behaved disgracefully with Basil. He could not forgive or forget. Certainly she had been a brick to-night. She was a queer mixture of good and bad. Sometimes he felt he could love her – other times he hated her.

'I don't know what I do feel. It's a beastly mix up!' he thought savagely, as he walked into his mother's room.

Stella lay perfectly still on the bed where he had laid her – too tired for thought – almost too tired to sleep. . . .

CHAPTER 9

An uneventful week followed Lady Eden's heart-attack. The old lady rallied and recovered completely. By the end of that week she was out of bed again and down in the sunlit garden, in her usual chair. Her devotion to Stella was more marked than ever.

'Pamela is a wonderful little nurse, Julian,' she told her son proudly. 'I don't know what she can't do.'

'She is certainly wonderful,' Julian agreed.

Mother and son were alone. Stella was in the garden with a basket and rose-clippers. She always changed and arranged the flowers for the house after breakfast.

'Her devotion to you is so exquisite,' added Lady Eden. 'You could not have married a better woman, Julian darling. You know, the modern woman does not make a good wife because she is so flighty and independent; but Pamela is neither of those things. She has no thought in life but you.'

Julian, smoking a pipe, looked out at the sunlit garden, his face blank.

'Do you really think that, Mother?' he asked curiously.

'I know it,' said Lady Eden. 'Only the other night, when she came to kiss me, she knelt by my bed, and said: 'Oh, Mother, I love him . . . I love him so. . . .' And I said: 'We both love him – we are both never done praising God for his return. . . .'

Julian's teeth clenched on the stem of his pipe. His cheeks flushed slightly.

Why should Stella have made that declaration of love? It

was unnecessary. Surely she need not act her part quite so well! It savoured rather of hypocrisy – and he did not like it.

'You love her just as much as she loves you, don't you, Julian?' he heard Lady Eden's soft voice.

'Why, yes, Mother,' he blurted out. 'Of course!'

Lady Eden reached out a hand and put it on his shoulder.

'Darling,' she said wistfully. 'The greatest desire of my life is to live long enough to see – a child of yours and Pamela's – play in this garden – a grandchild for me.'

This was more than Julian could stand. He averted his face, conscious that it was flaming.

'Yes, yes, Mother,' he stammered. 'I quite understand.'

'You aren't angry with me, dear – for saying that?'

'Angry? Good heavens, no! How could I be angry with you, sweet Mother?' he said with an embarrassed laugh. 'I understand. I – one never knows what might happen in this life! I – I think I'll go and help Pamela pick her flowers.'

Hurriedly he escaped. But not to join Stella. He could not face her now. His heart was pounding furiously, and his cheeks still scarlet with the confusion caused by his mother's words.

'A child!' he thought with bitter sarcasm. 'A child of mine – and hers! No . . . never . . . never.'

He would never know the joys of fatherhood. No son of his would ever play in the garden – perpetuate his name – inherit the old home.

There was strange anguish in that thought for Julian. By nature an affectionate, home-loving boy, he would have appreciated the joys of ordinary domesticity. And they were forever denied him. Pamela's desertion of him . . . Stella's impersonation . . . everything had ruined any such hopes of happiness that he might have entertained.

He avoided the rosery.

Had he passed that way he would have seen Stella sitting in the arbour; a basket of beautiful pink, scarlet and golden roses beside her; two letters in her hand.

One she had read. It was from Pamela; Pamela rhapsodising on the joys of life with Geoffrey in Paris!

'Every day makes me doubly realise my love for Geoff, and how utterly impossible it would be for me to break with him and return to Julian,' she had written. 'Go on with your game, I implore you, Stella darling – for my sake . . .'

Stella's grey eyes were full of bitterness when she lifted them from this note. Pamela was happy – careless of the fact that she was not Geoffrey's legal wife. She was happy – surrendering herself to his love . . . Lucky Pamela, to have no conscience – no regrets . . .

Reviewing this last week, Stella could feel nothing but regret. Julian had not mentioned the episode of Basil. He had been courteous and considerate to her. But he had been very cold. He practically ignored her when they were alone. Only in Lady Eden's presence did he make any effort to be the lover and the husband.

For those rare moments – when he pressed her hand or called her 'darling' – she was pathetically grateful. Her love for him seemed to increase each day.

To her mental anguish there seemed no end.

She sighed as she folded Pamela's letter and put it back in the envelope. Then she picked up the second letter. She did not recognise the writing. It bore the Lyndhurst post-mark.

The moment she had opened it and commenced to read the contents, however, she knew. A flush of anger and fear coloured her whole face. It was from Basil Hargreaves, Basil, who was apparently staying at the 'Crown.'

'I have not worried you this week because of Aunt Cecily's illness,' he wrote. 'But now, my fairest flower, I want to see you. You must meet me in the forest to-morrow afternoon. I insist! If you refuse, or tell Julian, the consequences be at your door.

'I shall expect you outside the 'Crown' at three o'clock, and we will stroll together to the woods.'

'B.H.'

Stella crushed the letter in her hands, her eyes blazing, her heart beating fast.

'How dare he?' she muttered. 'How dare he threaten me like this . . . the cur!'

But her anger and indignation soon evaporated. The old helpless feeling of the fly, caught in the spider's web, enveloped her. Basil held the upper hand. She knew that he was unscupulous enough to carry out his mean threat; to expose the truth to his aunt, should she either tell Julian, or refuse to meet him.

Fear, for Lady Eden's sake alone, led her to go to that assignation with Basil at three o'clock that afternoon. With guilt in her heart, and a feeling of misery, she had told Julian she was 'Going down to the village to 'shop'.'

Outside the 'Crown,' Basil was waiting – spruce and smiling.

'How sweet of you to come!' he murmured, as she reached him. 'I've been bored stiff this week – pottering about the place alone. And I've been thinking of you day and night, my lovely Stella. It does me good to see you again.'

She shrank back as he took her arm.

'It was mean and cowardly of you to force me to meet you,' she said. 'Why don't you behave like a decent gentleman and go back to Southampton – and leave me alone?'

'Because I'm too much in love with you, darling,' he said coolly. 'Now don't waste time lecturing me. Come along – we'll stroll into the forest and you can tell me how the situation progresses with my dear cousin.'

Reluctantly Stella went with him. He chatted to her all the way, keeping his desirous eyes on the slim, white-clad figure, and the beautiful, expressive face under the drooping brim of her big white hat.

Stella had felt sure that Julian would remain at Eden Hall that afternoon. He had complained of the heat, and suggested that he was going to sit under the chestnut-tree by the tennis-court and read.

But Julian changed his mind. While his mother was taking her afternoon nap, he decided to walk into the forest, find a cool spot there, and read.

The long arm of coincidence reached out and guided him to the exact part of the woods to which Basil Hargreaves had led Stella.

He came upon the couple suddenly. They neither saw nor heard him coming. They were sitting on a fallen log, half-hidden by a great spreading beech-tree.

He stopped dead; his lips tightening, his hands clenching at his sides.

'Stella – with Basil!' he muttered. 'My God! – I didn't think she was as bad as that. . . .'

He stood motionless for a moment. And suddenly Basil's voice reached him through the quiet of the forest.

'Now, don't be foolish, Stella. . . .'

Stella, Julian's cheeks whitened. So Basil knew that Stella was not Pamela Eden!

'Don't be foolish,' Basil continued. 'If you'd only try and care for me as much as I care for you, we could both be divinely happy.'

'I don't care and never shall. I loathe and despise you!' came Stella's voice, very clearly and decisively. 'If Julian knew that you were forcing me here – he'd want to murder you.'

'Julian has no claim – he is not your husband,' said Basil, with a sneering laugh.

'He is standing in the place of my husband,' answered Stella. 'And I'm supposed to be his wife. I simply cannot endure to be touched by you . . . and I've only come here this afternoon because I feared you might hurt Lady Eden. . . .'

Julian, straining his ears to listen, drew a sharp breath. The light of understanding was slowly dawning in his eyes. Stella was not wantonly flirting with Basil, nor even in love with him. She hated and despised him . . . he was forcing her here . . . apparently threatening to tell his aunt the truth, if she refused to meet him.

'I believe you are half in love with Julian,' Basil was saying now in a sardonic voice. 'Isn't that it?'

'I refuse to discuss him with you,' came Stella's reply. 'You are not worthy to speak his name.'

Julian flushed to the roots of his hair.

So that was how Stella felt about things – like *that* – she would not even discuss him. 'Half in love with him!' Was that so? Could it be . . .

But suddenly all other feelings save fury against his cousin, left Julian. He felt an almost murderous hate for the cad who had dared to threaten Stella.

Throwing back his head, he marched forward and faced the pair on the log.

They both sprang up – Stella dismayed – Basil dumbfounded at the unexpected apparition.

Julian walked up to his cousin.

'I've heard everything, Basil,' he said between clenched teeth. 'I know exactly what has been going on now, and how you have been terrorising Stella into meeting you, by threatening to tell mother the truth. Very well. Now you are going to pay for it. Get off your coat. I've got a very good ash-stick with me and I'm going to thrash you – thrash you within an inch of your life. . . .'

The coward in Basil Hargreaves swamped all other feelings as he looked into his cousin's flaming eyes. He licked his lips nervously and moved back a pace.

'D-don't be stupid, Julian!' he stuttered.

'Stupid!' Julian gave a harsh laugh. 'That's the wrong word. I should consider myself stupid if I let you go scot-free. Take off your coat!'

Stella, who had been watching the two men with breathless interest, felt suddenly afraid – not for Basil's sake; he deserved a thrashing; but for Julian's sake. He was in a blind rage – he might do his cousin serious injury and regret it afterwards. She sprang to his side and caught his arm.

'Julian – is it worth it?' she panted. 'I know he is an absolute cur, but –'

'Don't ask me to show any mercy,' Julian cut in roughly. 'he *is* a cur, and by Heaven, curs were meant to be thrashed! He has made your life miserable. He is not going to be let off.'

'See here, two can play at this game,' Basil began with a weak laugh, throwing off his coat. 'I'll fight with you.'

'Come on, then!' said Julian. He took off his own coat and flung it to the ground, together with his stick. 'Fight if you want to. . . .'

Stella moved back and leaned against a tree, her hand pressed to her palpitating heart, her cheeks hot. She felt a queer, primitive pleasure in the sight of these two male creatures fighting before her. She looked at Basil, who was sickly pale and making a poor pretence at defiance; then at Julian. Ah, Julian was splendid! Head thrown back, shoulders squared; sleeves rolled back, showing the rippling muscles of his forearms, His were the tight lips, the narrowed, fiercely-watchful eyes of the fighter.

Stella could not take her eyes off Julian. She felt, somehow, that he was fighting for *her;* fighting because Basil had 'made her life miserable' – and he resented it. Surely that proved he did not hate her quite so much. Besides, he knew the truth now – knew that she had not wantonly flirted with Basil that night, a week ago.

Julian and his cousin were grappling with each other now. Basil hit out blindly – wildly. But Julian had taken boxing lessons in his college days. He was not so slim nor perhaps so nimble as Basil, but he understood the art of boxing, and he was easily the victor. Within five minutes he had landed a left and a right to Basil's jaw that laid the younger man on the ground.

Basil lay face downwards, his shoulders heaving, his breath coming in sobbing gasps.

Julian picked up the stick.

'You've had your chance to fight – and lost,' he said between his clenched teeth. 'Now will you take your thrashing?'

Basil rolled over and sat up. He was craven – pallid – shaking.

'Let me alone!' he said hoarsely.

'Yes, let him go, Julian,' put in Stella.

Julian turned and looked at her.

'Women are soft-hearted creatures,' he said with a curt laugh. 'They always end by pleading for the cads who had been brutes to them. No, Stella, I am not going to let my charming cousin go – yet. This will, I hope be a lesson that he won't quickly forget.

'W-what r-right have you got to – to c-criticise me?' came from Basil, in a stammering voice. 'You have p-pretended Stella is your wife. That's not b-behaving in the r-right way, is it?'

'I don't intend to discuss my affairs with you,' said Julian. 'In any case, you had made up your mind to make love to the woman you believed to be my wife before you knew she was not. It's about time you learned not to poach on other men's preserves.'

Basil had stumbled on to his feet. He stood there swaying – his eyes full of fear – his mouth gaping loosely. He was not a pretty sight, and Stella shuddered and turned her eyes from him.

She leaned against the tree, covering her face with her hands. She did not see what followed, but she *heard* . . . heard the dull thud of a stick across Basil's back – heard the man's hoarse cry of pain – then another – and another . . . until the cries became sobbing moans and appeals for mercy.

She felt at last that she could stand no more. She lifted her head and looked at Julian.

'*That,* for your threats to hurt mother!' Julian was snarling. '*That*, for your treatment of Stella – you hound!'

'Stop, Julian!' Stella gasped. 'Stop – for heaven's sake! You'll kill him!'

Julian – stick suspended in the air – met her gaze; then looked at his cousin, who was a limp, groaning thing in his grasp. The hot temper that had boiled over within him seemed to cool down – and suddenly he released Basil and pitched the stick away from him.

Basil tottered on his feet a moment, then collapsed in a heap on the ground. He lay there with his face hidden. His collar had been ripped from the studs; his shirt was torn; there was blood on it where the stick had broken the skin.

Stella felt sick and faint as she looked down at him. But Julian, as he put on his coat and smoothed back his hair, smiled grimly.

'I feel better – much better,' he said.

'Are you going to – leave him here?' Stella faltered.

'Certainly,' said Julian. 'When he feels like it he can find his way home.'

He bent over his cousin.

'Listen to me, Basil,' he said. 'You've had your punishment, and I trust you won't forget it. If you write to mother or make her in the least degree suspicious that Stella is not my wife, I'll kill you. Do you hear? I'll thrash you again – and thrash you till you die! *Do you hear?*'

Basil stirred and groaned.

'Yes, I hear,' he mumbled.

'Get back to the 'Crown' and explain your condition as best you can,' added Julian. 'And I give you until this evening to leave the district. Dare to come back to the New Forest, and you know what to expect. Is that understood?'

'Yes,' muttered Basil.

Julian looked at Stella.

'Come,' he said. 'We'll get along home.'

Stella gave a last, sickened look at the man on the

ground, then turned and walked with Julian back toward Eden Hall.

Glancing at her wrist-watch, she saw that the time was half-past four – an hour-and-a-half had gone by since she started out to meet Basil in Lyndhurst village. Enormous relief surged through her as she silently walked beside the man she loved.

Her sensations when she had gone to that enforced meeting with Basil had been very different. She had been frightened, depressed, hopeless. Now everything had changed. She need no longer be afraid of Basil and his threats, nor tortured by his love-making. And best of all, she knew that Julian could no longer think of her as a despicable flirt. He had said nothing. He was keeping silence. But he would say something to her, later – she felt sure. Her heart beat fast with anticipation.

She never forgot that homeward walk through the forest. The late afternoon sun slanted goldenly through the green lace of the leafy trees. It was cool and dim and restful. A peace such as she had not known for long days and nights, came now to Stella.

Just before they reached the fringe of the forest and came out on the main road, Julian broke the silence. He paused and turned to the girl.

'Stella,' he said, in a queer voice, 'I want to talk to you for a moment.'

'Yes,' she said.

'I don't quite know what to say,' he went on, looking down at the ground. 'I'm not very good at making speeches.'

'Is it necessary for you to make a speech?' she asked.

He looked up at her swiftly and met her timid smile. He read tenderness, sympathy, infinite sweetness in that smile. He felt that he had never seen anything more beautiful. His old antagonism toward her; his belief that she was mercenary and scheming, were swept away on a sudden tide of understanding – of admiration for her.

'Oh, my dear!' he said huskily. 'It is necessay for me to tell you how much I think of you for – for doing whatever you have done. You sacrificed yourself for my mother . . . you allowed me to say bitter, outrageous things to you, that night when I turned Basil out of the house . . . and all because you were afraid he might tell mother the truth!'

'Yes, I know,' said Stella, her face flooding with colour. 'But – I couldn't have let him disillusion mother. She is so happy in the belief that I am your wife.'

'You have behaved in a very noble and wonderful way,' said Julian. 'I want to thank you . . . and to apologise.'

'Oh, why apologise?' she cried.

'For all the beastly things I said to you.'

'You thought I deserved them,' she said.

'But I know now that you did not. I also know that your love for my mother is very genuine and very fine. I thank you for that.'

'I don't want to be thanked,' she said, feeling very embarrassed. 'I do love Lady Eden with all my heart, and not for worlds would I have let Basil hurt her.'

'Basil!' Julian ground his teeth. 'The skunk! I feel I could go back and thrash him again.'

'No, no! You punished him sufficiently, I feel sure,' said Stella.

'What luck I found you!' said Julian. 'Extraordinary luck! If I hadn't found you, I suppose you would never have told me.'

'I don't suppose I should. He said he would tell your mother at once, if I gave him away to you.'

'And you would have gone on meeting him – suffering his beastly attentions – risking my anger and contempt – until further notice?'

Stella looked away from him and laughed nervously.

'Oh, yes, I daresay. But please don't let's talk about it any more. It's all over now.'

Julian reached out a hand and gripped hers.

'You're a fine woman, Stella,' he said – 'the finest I've ever met. Please forgive me for all the brutal things I've ever said or done to you.'

'You have not been brutal at all,' she said.

Her hand quivered slightly in his. He, watching her, saw her beautiful face flushing and paling alternately; and could not help but realise, now, that there was something behind her noble actions – something besides her love for his mother. He remembered Basil's cynical remark: 'I believe you are half in love with Julian . . . ' and remembered her reply: 'I refuse to discuss him with you. You are not worthy to speak his name . . . '

Did Stella love him?

The idea shook him from head to foot. He caught his lower lip between his teeth.

'Julian, we must get back to mother,' he heard the girl say in her soft voice. 'We are very late for tea.'

That made him recover his equilibrium. He pressed her hand tightly, then dropped it.

'Yes, you are right,' he said. 'Come along.'

They continued the walk in silence. Stella – hand hurting from the strong grip of Julian's fingers – looked ahead with radiant eyes. She was filled with sheer happiness, because things were right between them now, and he no longer hated her.

But the man's face was puckered with troubled thought. This affair was developing in an astonishing way of which he had not dreamed. He was obsessed now by the idea that Stella cared for him. And he . . . he was not at all sure that he was not in love with her. In love with the woman who was impersonating his wife . . . and his real wife in Paris, with another man!

What an awful muddle! What a position for them all to be in.

Julian's thoughts and emotions, by the time he reached home, were in chaos.

CHAPTER 10

That same evening, Stella dressed for dinner with meticulous care. Why – she hardly knew; except that at the back of her head was the desire to look nice for Julian.

The rest of the afternoon had passed uneventfully. They had had tea out on the lawn, and Julian had behaved in a natural manner – only rather more light-heartedly than usual.

'My boy's getting back some of his spirits, Pamela,' Lady Eden had said to Stella. 'He has been rather depressed lately – and little wonder! It will take him some time to forget that terrible accident. But he is much brighter today.'

Stella had said nothing. But she had thought rather guiltily of the episode in the forest. What would Lady Eden have said had she known that Julian had thrashed her nephew within an inch of his life?

Having vented his feelings on Basil, no doubt Julian did feel better and brighter. It had been an outlet for his doubting, bitter, troubled mood of the last week.

Stella looked at her reflection in the mirror just before she went downstairs. She was surprised at her own beauty. She had put on black lace demi toilette, with long floating wings of chiffon from each shoulder. It was a graceful frock, and suited her slenderness. Her arms and throat gleamed like ivory; her usually pale face was delicately flushed; her grey eyes bright.

'Why do I look like this to-night?' she asked herself. 'Why do I feel so extraordinarily happy?'

There was no real reason. The position was as intolerable as ever. Yet somehow she felt undisturbed; she felt, as she walked down to the drawing-room, that she was indeed Mrs. Julian Eden – mistress of this beautiful home – serene – at peace with the world.

Lady Eden was still in her bedroom; and Julian had not finished dressing, so Stella found herself alone.

She walked up to the grand piano. It had not been opened since her arrival. She loved music, and was filled with a sudden desire to revive her playing and singing. She sat down on the stool and ran her fingers over the keyboard.

'How stiff I am!' she thought. 'I can't play a note!'

Julian, up in his dressing-room, heard the strains of music floating up to him, and paused in the act of brushing his hair, to listen.

'Stella playing,' he said to himself. 'I didn't know she played the piano. She's rather good at it.'

He was discovering that Stella was good at many things. Altogether, she was becoming of vast interest to him. He completed his toilet, slipped into his dinner-jacket, and walked downstairs. Outside the drawing-room he paused. Stella was singing. She had one of those low, sweet voices – quite untrained, but very sympathetic and true. Her diction was good, too, and Julian could hear every word she sang – a charming little love-song which had been a great favourite of hers in the past.

'Summer, summer, must you go?
For two of us have loved you so!
Loved you in your hours of rain,
And loved you when you smiled again. . . .'

Julian softly opened the door and tiptoed into the room. He tried to sit down without being seen by the pianist, but Stella saw him at once and stopped singing.

'Now, don't do that,' he said. 'Go on – please.'

'I never sing in public,' she protested. 'I – my fingers are frightfully stiff and my voice is husky. Do you know, I haven't sung a note since our old home broke up, and Pamela and I started to earn our livings.'

'Never mind. I listened upstairs and enjoyed it,' said Julian. 'Please finish that song. What is it?'

'Two of Us,' by Lyall-Phillips,' she said. 'It is very sweet. I have always loved it.'

'Finish it,' he repeated.

'Stella's heart beat swiftly. She gave a nervous little laugh.

Oh – very well!' she said.

Julian sat back in his chair and smoked. His eyes closed as the girl began the second verse:

'Summer, summer, when you fly,
Two of us, must say goodbye.
Never sunshine, never rain
Will fall on just we two again
Soon the autumn winds will sigh
And soon the crimson roses die.
Oh, summer, summer, did you know
Two of us have loved you so?'

The plaintive tune, the words – so full of pathos – so expressive of a breaking heart, touched Julian deeply. He opened his eyes and looked at Stella. She was sitting with her hands loosely locked in her lap, her dark head bowed. There were tears on her cheeks.

He felt his heart give a quick jerk – then beat on more swiftly. His throat felt dry. Why was she crying? Why was she so unhappy? Did she feel that when this summer ended, she would probably say good-bye to him . . . that things would pan out so that it would no longer be necessary for her to impersonate his wife, and she would go away?

'Never sunshine, never rain
Will fall on just we two again. . . .'

Those words reiterated in his brain.

He suddenly rose and crossed to the piano.

'Stella?' he said. He was surprised to hear his voice shaking.

She looked up at him quickly.

'Yes?'

'Are you unhappy?'

'Why do you ask?' She swallowed hard.

'Because you sang as though you were desperately miserable. Have I made you very miserable? Have I been very unkind to you?'

'No, or course not. But you know you have said many times that I deserved any punishment you chose to mete out to me.'

He reddened and pitched his cigarette into the empty grate. He looked from the girl out of the window. Dusk was veiling the garden. The fringe of the forest was just visible through the blue mist. Inexplicable sadness was gripping him – he scarcely knew why – and an inexplicable desire to take Stella in his arms and kiss those tears from her cheeks and curving lashes.

'I have said some very hard things to you,' at length he broke the silence between them. 'But as I told you in the forest to-day, I did not know you then as well as I know you now. I've realised to-day how unjust I've been in my criticism – how much too ready to condemn you. I think that when you came here and posed as my widow, it was entirely for my mother's sake.'

Her heart missed a beat. She looked at him with shining eyes.

'You really think that?'

'I do.'

'Then I am not in the least unhappy any longer,' she said.

'I have been wretched – I admit it – because I felt that you hated and despised me. Now that I know you understand my motives for doing the wrong I did – I am happy.'

'Have you cared so much what I thought about you?'

Stella caught her breath.

'Oh – you – what right have you to ask that?' she returned, a deep flush staining her throat and neck.

'None,' he said unsteadily. 'I – I beg your pardon. I – I think I'm feeling a little crazy to-night.'

'We all feel like that at times,' she said, twisting her handkerchief into a ball.

The door opened. Lady Eden came slowly into the room, on Hannah's arm.

'There you are, you two dear children,' she said. 'Have I kept you waiting for dinner?' The gong has only just gone, though, I think.

With an extraordinarily guilty feeling, Julian and Stella moved apart and walked with the old lady into the dining-room. They had neither of them heard the gong.

During dinner, Stella felt a strange, breathless excitement. She talked volubly to Lady Eden. And all the time she was conscious of Julian's scrutiny. Every time she dared look at him, she saw his vivid blue eyes fixed on her, and she blushed like a young girl in the presence of her first lover.

Those blushes seemed to go to Julian's head like wine.

'How adorable she is!' he told himself. 'I must have been blind and mad not to realise it before. She is ten times more attractive than Pamela could ever be.'

Pamela! He seemed to have forgotten the existence of the frivolous, faithless little wife who was now living with another man in Paris. He could only think of this dark-haired, grey-eyed girl who sat opposite him at dinner; who wore the wedding-ring he had placed on Pamela's finger; who had proved herself worthy of the name Eden – far more worthy than Pamela. Pamela would never have made any sacrifice for her mother-in-law. She was not that sort – she was far too wrapped up in herself.

Julian insisted upon more music, after dinner. Lady Eden retired early, as usual, and left the young people alone.

Julian went upstairs with his mother. When he came down, it was just in time to hear the finish of another song from Stella.

'If aught that I have told you
Should cause one moment's pain,
Love, I will take and hold you
Within my arms again. . . .
And fold you quickly to my heart before we part. . . .
Then let us say it quickly, you and I –
Goody-bye!'

Her soft voice died away. She rose from the piano-stool and came towards Julian, her cheeks like poppies, her eyes very bright.

'Well, I am tired,' she said. 'Then let us say it quickly, you and I – good night,' she parodied the song, laughing.

But as she looked up into the man's eyes, her laughter died away. She saw a look in those eyes that she had never dreamed that she would see. It held her spell-bound – filled her with astonishment and with an almost terrible ectasy.

Julian was falling in love with her. . . .*he had fallen in love!* She could see it – she could not help knowing it. . . .

And then, before she could move or break the spell, he had taken her in his arms. He held her against him in a fierce, passionate clasp, and set his lips to hers.

That long, deep kiss drove every ounce of strength from Stella's body. With closed eyes and pale face she lay in his arms, her lips locked to his – her arms about his throat.

It seemed a long, long time before he lifted his mouth from hers. She felt that during that kiss she had given herself to him utterly. He must know that she belonged to him – body and soul – that she had always loved him. And she was gloriously unashamed and glad. Because he loved her; the burning pressure of his lips told her so. He had kissed her before; kissed her with brutal passion – with the desire for revenge. But this was different. There was a new quality in his kiss, his clasp of her – the quality of tenderness, of reverence; of all, combined with passion, that a man shows to the woman he loves.

At last Julian raised his head. He drew a deep breath and looked down at her. She opened her eyes and smiled up at him.

'My dear!' he said huskily. 'My dearest. . . .'

'Julian, what has come over us?' she whispered.

'The most wonderful thing in the world,' he said. 'I have discovered that I love you.'

She thrilled from head to foot. Her arms tightened about him.

'You mean that?'

'You know it,' he said. 'I love you – love you, my dear, as I have never loved a woman before. And you love me. You need not tell me so.'

'But I want to,' she said. 'I am so proud of it. Ah, Julian, I have loved you from the very beginning.'

'What! When I was so cruel to you – so beastly – so absolutely *beastly?*'

'Yes, even then,' she said gravely. 'I loved you before you came home, you see. During those days when I first came to Eden Hall, I heard so much about you – I grew so familiar with your photographs – I learned to love the memory of you. When I saw the real Julian, I loved him. Your brutalities I deserved, for impersonating Pamela.'

'No,' he said. 'You deserved nothing but my gratitude for your devotion to my mother. Only I was a mad fool – bitter and cynical because of Pamela's desertion of me.'

Suddenly Stella shivered.

'Oh, Julian!' she said. 'Julian!'

He held her closer.

'What, what, my darling?'

'Pamela is – still your wife.'

'No!' he said roughly. 'She is Geoffrey Raynes' wife. She is not mine any longer.'

'By law she is,' insisted Stella. 'You have no right to love me. Neither have I any right to love you.'

'But I do,' he said, triumph in his voice. 'I love you, I love you,' he repeated.

The joy of being loved by this man whom she had loved so long and hopelessly, blotted out the remembrance of Pamela for a few moments.

She drew his handsome head down to hers.

'Oh, my dear – my love of loves!' she said passionately.

Their lips met and clung in another breathless, flaming kiss. And this time, when the kiss ended, Julian's lips sought her eyes, her hair, her cheeks, her throat. She surrendered to him, all the pent-up passion and longing of the past finding an outlet at last.

He drew her down on the sofa, still holding her in his arms.

'I must arrange a divorce – a divorce between Pamela and myself,' he said. 'She is happy with Raynes. She must stay with him – and I must marry you.'

'How can that be arranged without Geoffrey learning the truth?'

'How can that be arranged without Geoffrey learning the truth?'

'I don't know. But we must find a way. I love you madly, Stella, and I can't live like this any longer – just acting a part.'

She met his passionate eyes, and her head drooped a little.

'My lovely, wonderful girl! My dearest. . . .'

There came a knock at the drawing-room door.

Stella drew away from Julian and patted her hair into order.

'See who it is, Julian,' she whispered.

The man walked to the door and opened it. A maid stood outside, holding a telegram in her hand.

'A wire for Mrs. Eden, sir,' she said.

A strange premonition of disaster seized Stella as she ripped open the envelope.

'Oh, my God!' she said. 'Read it, Julian.'

He took it from her.

'Geoffrey in a taxi-accident this morning. He died this afternoon. I am nearly mad. Come to me.

'PAMELA.'

Julian read Pamela's telelgram twice – then he crumpled it up in his hand and looked at Stella.

They stared at each other speechlessly for a moment. It was Stella who broke the silence.

'Oh, Julian – how terrible – how terrible for her!'

'I don't know what to say,' he murmured. 'I feel absolutely shattered by this.'

'My poor little Pam,' said Stella. 'She says she is nearly mad. Of course I must go to her. I must go to Paris at once, Julian – first thing in the morning.'

Julian's heart sank.

'Must you? Oh, my dear –'

'You know I don't want to leave you,' broke in Stella, in an agitated voice. 'But I must go to Pam. She is my baby-sister – I've always loved her and looked after her like a mother, Julian. She needs me. Look here – let me scribble a reply to Pam, and let Edith take it.'

'We haven't a telegraph form in the house,' said Julian mechanically. 'But I daresay the boy will have one on him.'

He summoned Edith, who procured the necessary form. Stella sent her reply:

'Coming to you to-morrow. – STELLA.'

She addressed it to 'Mrs. Geoffrey Raynes, Hotel Maurice, Paris.'

After Edith had gone, and she was alone again with Julian, Stella broken down. She leaned her head on her arm and sobbed bitterly.

'My poor Pam – my poor little Pam!' she kept on saying. 'And poor, poor Geoffrey! Julian, you may feel bitter about Pam, but you would have liked Geoff – he was one of the best – a real white man – and Pam loved him. I'm sure she loved him.'

'She loved me once,' said Julian, his lips compressed. 'I don't believe in Pamela's loves. She gives way to the passion of the moment. But anyhow, this is a ghastly business. The poor chap – killed in an accident – on his honeymoon. It is awful!'

'Thank God he died in happy ignorance,' said Stella, her face streaming with tears. 'It would have broken his heart to learn the truth.'

Julian sat down on the sofa and drew the girl into his arms. Gently he laid his cheek against hers, moving his lips now and then to kiss away the tears.

'My tender-hearted Stella,' he whispered. 'Always thinking of others – never of herself!'

'That's not true,' said Stella, wiping her eyes. 'I'm horribly selfish.'

'I don't think so. I think you are the most unselfish and wonderful woman I have ever met,' he said. He gave a deep sigh. For a moment she pressed her face to his; then she put her arms around his neck and looked deeply, anxiously into his eyes.

'Julian,' she said, 'this terrible thing that has happened in

Paris is going to make all the difference to *us.*'

Julian felt a queer constriction of the throat. He did not answer. But he held Stella a little closer to him, as though afraid to let that warm sweet presence go from him.

'All the difference,' repeated Stella. 'Indeed, it seems that Fate has decided for us, Julian.'

'What do you mean?' he asked. His voice was hoarse. 'Decided what?'

'That you and I can never be together,' she said.

'My God – I can't – I won't accept that!'

'My dear, my dear,' she said, smoothing back his hair. 'How can we marry now? Pamela is – by law – neither wife nor widow of poor Geoffrey's. She must revert to her old position – as Mrs. Julian Eden.'

'No – never!' said Julian, between his teeth.

'But she must – she has nobody else to come to in the world – but me. And how can she come here as Geoffrey's widow? It would be ludicrous!'

'She mustn't come here at all,' said Julian. 'All our efforts to keep the truth from mother would have been useless, if Pamela came now and spoilt everything.'

Stella bit her lip.

'Yes – I know. Mother must not learn the truth,' she nodded. 'But, my dear, this is a terrible problem. I can't think what to say or do.'

'Nor I,' said Julian, in a tone of despair. 'I've never felt more perplexed.'

'A good deal depends on what Pamela has to say,' went on Stella. 'I don't know yet what she means to do.'

Julian suddenly released Stella, and, leaning forward, put his head between his hands.

'What a damnable state of affairs!' he muttered. 'Everything would have been all right, if Raynes had lived. I could have managed somehow to get a divorce from Pamela, and marry you. But now – well, even now, why can't we readjust things?' he added, looking up at Stella defiantly. We can't live our lives apart.'

The girl swallowed hard. With tear-blurred eyes she stared at him. Every feature of the strong, handsome face was so dear and familiar to her – the rough, dark hair; the vividly blue eyes. She loved and worshipped him. And now that she knew he cared for her, it was going to make things doubly hard. How *could* they live their lives apart?

'My dear,' she said. 'My dearest, what *can* we do?'

He drew her back into his arms with a fierce little gesture.

'We must do something,' he said. 'When Pamela comes back to England I must see her and tell her outright that I care for you – ask her to divorce me. Mother need never know; and you and I could be quietly married and just come back here as though nothing had ever happened.'

Stella began to tremble. She clung to Julian and pressed her troubled face against his shoulder.

'How can that be managed? What reason has Pam to divorce you?'

'Because I shall refuse to live with her.'

'If you started a law-suit it would get into the papers – the truth would come out – everybody would know I'd been impersonating Pam;'

'It's the very dickens!' said Julian, with a hopeless shrug of his shoulders. 'I can't think what to do – for the best. I only know that I love you, Stella, and I shall never live with any other woman in the world.'

'My darling!' she murmured.

He put his hands under her chin and lifted her face up to his. His lips covered her mouth. For a moment they clung together in a passionate, desperate embrace.

At last Stella drew back. Her beautiful grey eyes closed wearily.

'I love you so, Julian,' she whispered. 'Much too much, in fact.'

'You could never love me enough,' he said, keeping her hands in his and kissing them each in turn.

'Because I love you so much, my darling, that I need all

your love in return.'

'You have it,' she said. 'You have always had it. But it is wrong. You are my sisters's husband. It is wrong from beginning to end.'

'Real love cannot be wrong,' argued Julian.

'Ah, but it can, dear!' said Stella, shaking her head. 'And the first thing necessary to real love is a sense of honour and duty. We must be honourable – we must play the game, Julian.'

'My dear, you are a very, very good woman,' he said. 'I can't think how I ever imagined you to be otherwise.'

'Oh, but I did great wrong in coming here as your wife!' said the girl, in a passionate undertone. 'If I hadn't come, there would not have been such terrible trouble now. Pam might have married Geoff just the same, but that could perhaps have been rectified. Now – there is nothing but trouble ahead. Everybody in Lyndhurst believes me to be Mrs. Eden.'

'I wish to heaven you were!' said Julian. 'My love, my love!' He hid his face on her breast.

She smoothed his hair with tender hands.

'My poor Julian,' she said. 'You are worried to death.'

'I love you. I want you,' he said under his breath. His arms were folded about her, holding tightly against him. 'Stella, Stella, what are we going to do?'

'Wait until I've been to Paris,' she said. 'I must see Pam and hear what she has to say, Julian. Once you loved Pam – you married her secretly – you must have loved her very much. Have you no feelings of affection left for her?'

'None,' he said, in a muffled tone. 'I was infatuated with Pam, and married her in the heat of the moment. After my accident I felt a passionate longing to see her and hold her in my arms again. I built up an ideal – pictured a faithful, sorrowing little wife waiting for me. When I heard that she had married again within a year, and had never really cared for me, all my desire to see her again seemed to die –

completely. I saw just what a foolish marriage mine had been. And now that I have learned to love *you* I think myself doubly a fool for having plunged into matrimony with her.'

Stella nodded. She continued to stroke his head without speaking for a moment; her brows knit in thought. Then she said:

'Well, my dear one, there is nothing to be done now. We cannot possibly come to any conclusion. I shall join Pam in Paris to-morrow. I shall tell mother that my sister has lost her husband in an accident, and needs me – and she will understand.'

'Perhaps she'll suggest that I should take you over,' said Julian, raising his head and looking at Stella with strained eyes. 'But I must refuse . . . say that I wish to remain with her.'

'Yes, you mustn't come with me,' Stella said. 'But I'll write to you, Julian, and tell you what Pam decides to do.'

'Whatever that may be, swear that you won't let mother suffer,' said Julian.

'You know you can rely on that, my dear.'

'Yes, I believe in you implicitly,' he said.

'Poor little Pam – and poor Geoffrey!' sighed Stella.

'I'll go to town very early, in order to catch the second boat-train to Dover.'

'Tell me again that you love me, Stella,' said Julian huskily.

She put her arms about his neck and surrendered to his hands and lips completely for a few moments.

'I love you – I love you, Julian,' she said. 'God be merciful to us, my dear – but it is a terrible tangle to unravel.'

'I love you, my darling,' he said, holding her closely to him. 'Whatever happens, nothing can take my love from you.'

'Nor mine from you,' she whispered. 'Good night, good

night, my dearest.'

'Good night, and God bless you, darling,' he said.

Their lips met and clung in a long, long kiss.

CHAPTER 11

The following evening, about seven o'clock, Stella walked into the Raynes' private sitting-room at the Hotel Maurice, Paris.'

'Madame is distraught,' the kind-hearted little French maid, who looked after that particular suite, informed Stella, as she conducted her to Pamela. 'I am very glad Madame's sister has come . . . *mon Dieu! C'est terrible!* . . .'

Yes. It was terrible. Stella seemed to forget everything in the world but overwhelming love and compassion for Pamela, when she saw the girl. Already in deep mourning, Pamela rose from the depths of a chair to greet her sister. Stella caught a glimpse of a white, pinched little face and two tragic eyes; then Pamela was in her arms, clinging to her, sobbing.

'Stella, Stella . . . thank God you've come! I've gone nearly mad. Oh, Stella, my poor Geoff – my poor, poor Geoff!'

Stella held her tightly, drew her down on to the couch and sat with the girl in her arms rocking her to and fro as she would have rocked a baby. Never had Pam been more dear to her; never had she seemed more pathetic, more helpless and sorrowful. She kissed the golden head, her own eyes blinded with tears.

'It is cruel, Pam – I know it is cruel. You loved him. Poor Geoffrey – poor, poor Geoffrey, and poor you!'

'He was so young to die,' sobbed Pamela. 'And so much in love with life – with me. Our honeymoon was such a glorious thing, Stella! Even the fact that Julian returned from the dead hardly marred my happiness with Geoff.'

'Darling, try to be brave,' said Stella. 'It is easy to preach – hard to carry out what one preaches, and yet I do feel that courage is the only thing left to one if one loses one's beloved. *He* would rather feel you are bearing his loss bravely.'

Pamela tore herself from her sister's arms, and buried her head in the cushions, crying tempestuously.

'Why did God take him? It is unfair – unjust! Oh, I can't bear it – I can't bear it!'

Stella wiped her eyes, and drew a long, weary breath. She thought perhaps it were better to let Pamela cry out her grief. Poor little Pam! The first sharp pangs of bitter anguish when death takes a loved one are indeed hard to bear.

She visualised herself losing Julian – had she been his wife – and she shuddered.

She removed her hat and coat and gloves, and looked round a moment at the room. It was a typical French apartment, very elegantly appointed, and there were masses of flowers everywhere. Probably poor Geoffrey had brought his bride those flowers.

Somehow, Stella could not help being glad for Geoffrey's own sake that he had died ere he had discovered the truth about the girl he had married. He would have been so terribly hurt to learn that she had already been a wife; that she had wilfully deceived him.

Yet he might have forgiven her. She was so young – a broken, helpless child, to-day, anyhow. Who would have the heart to reproach her for any wrong thing she had done?

'I shall never, never be happy again – never love a man again,' came Pamela's voice – hoarse and muffled in the cushion. 'Oh, Stella, I feel I don't want to live! I've nothing to live for.'

'Nonsense, dear!' said Stella, gently, putting an arm about the quivering figure. 'You have all your life before you.'

'You don't know what love is, then, if you can talk like that!' said Pamela, in a passionate tone.

Stella closed her eyes. Not know, what love is, she, who loved Julian Eden so madly, so desperately! Ah, Pam did not know about that *yet* . . .

'My dear,' she said. 'Believe me – you will get over poor Geoffrey's death. Time is a great healer.'

'Time will never heal *my* wound,' sobbed the girl.

A sharp stab went through Stella's heart. She suddenly sat up and clenched her hands in her lap. For she remembered . ... history was repeating itself . . . she had heard Pamela say those words before . . . 'Time will never, never heal my wound!' Yes, Pamela had said that when the news of Julian's accident had reached her. Stella had a vivid mental picture of that day, not long ago after all, when Pamela had sobbed in her arms as passionately as she was sobbing now. She had loved her first husband; she had said nothing could make her happy again.

Yet within twelve months, she had fogotten her love, and conceived a great passion for Geoffrey Raynes.

Stella shook her head sadly as she looked at her sister. Poor Pam! She was incapable of real, great love – of real, great grief. Her passions, her sorrows, were superficial. Yet they hurt her at the time. Stella gave her the benefit of that doubt. She knew Pam's character so well. Pam suffered real anguish in her own way. But it was passing. Everything with her was passing . . . .

'Pam, darling,' she said, bending over the girl, 'try and believe me when I tell you that you will get over this. I hardly like to speak of Julian now – yet you loved him once and grieved at his death, didn't you, Pamela?'

Pamela ceased crying. She sat up, pressing a tear-soaked handkerchief to her swollen eyes. She looked with indignation at her sister.

'You know I never cared for Julian like I cared for Geoff!'

'Perhaps not,' said Stella quietly. 'Only you, yourself, can be judge of that.'

Pamela's face flooded with hot colour.

'I don't want to speak of Julian,' she said in a suffocating voice. 'The whole situation is too abominable.'

'Then let us speak of the immediate future,' said Stella. 'What are you going to do, Pam?'

'Geoffrey is – is at the hospital to which he was taken and where he died,' said Pamela, presssing her hands to her eyes. 'He was going to the bank to cash a cheque, Stella', and his taxi collided with a private car. He was terribly injured – his chest was crushed – but he lived long enough to say good-bye to – to me when they sent for me.'

Stella drew the girl into her arms.

'My poor darling!' she whispered.

'He was so sweet – so trustful – always,' said Pamela, chokingly. 'I shall never, *never* forget him!'

'Don't – there is no reason why you should, dear,' said Stella. 'Think of him and your brief honeymoon always as the golden summer of your life.'

'The – funeral will be to-morrow,' said Pamela, shuddering. 'You must come with me, Stella.'

'Of course. They are burying him in Paris, then?'

'Yes, I thought it best to – get it over – at once.'

'You are very wise,' nodded Stella. 'And after that, dearest, what do you mean to do?'

'I scarcely know,' said Pamela. 'I – I'm quite independent, of course. As Geoffrey's widow, I – get everything, and he was rich, Stella.'

'I am thankful you will never want, dear,' said the elder girl quietly. 'But now, Pamela we *must* speak of Julian. There are serious things to be faced . . . it is useless beating about the bush and postponing the conversation.'

A curiously sullen look came over Pamela's face – a pretty face still, despite the blotches caused by her violent weeping.

'Well? What about Julian?'

'Try and remember, Pamela, that you are – still his wife. The world may think you poor Geoffrey's widow. But you are not . . . you are *Julian's* wife!'

Pamela's eyes narrowed. She clasped her hands about her knees.

'Yes I understand that. But I refuse to call myself Julian's wife.'

Stella felt her heart miss a beat.

'You mean to – get a divorce, than?'

'Why not?' Pamela shrugged her shoulders. 'I must see him – talk it over with him quite calmly and dispassionately.'

'When, Pamela?'

'I shall come to England with you after my poor darling's funeral. Than I shall accompany you to Lyndhurst.'

'I'd rather you didn't, Pam.'

'Why not?' asked Pamela, defiantly.

'Don't you understand the situation down there in Eden Hall?' asked Stella, her face flushed with painful colour. 'Lady Eden believed me to be *you.*'

'Yes. I know that. It is amazing,' said Pamela. She eyed her sister much as she would have eyed a complete stranger. 'To think of *you* doing that, Stella!'

'I did it for Lady Eden's sake Pam. She was so old and frail and broken-hearted – she needed my love.'

'It would have been all right had Julian never returned,' muttered Pamela. 'Heavens! What a muddle you must all have been in!'

'It was pretty awful,' said Stella, with a short laugh, 'and many things have happened that I've not told you – because I didn't want to worry you.'

Pamela stared into her sister's face. Stella did not meet

her gaze, and after a moment Pamela bit her lips and nodded.

'H'm,' she said in a queer voice. 'I guessed as much. You've fallen in love with Julian, Stella.'

Stella swallowed hard. Then she tilted her head with a proud little gesture.

'Yes, I won't deceive you, Pamela. I *do* love Julian – and – *he loves me.*'

Pamela gave a hysterical laugh.

'What a situation! My husband and my sister – in love with each other!'

'It is all wrong – I know,' said Stella, trembling. 'And it has got to stop.'

'Do you love Julian very much, Stella?'

'Yes, with all my heart and all my soul.'

'What is he like now?'

'He is a very fine man, Pamela – both to look at and to speak to.'

'He was always very handsome,' said Pamela, reflectively. 'And a clever boy, too.'

'He is not a boy now. He has become a man – and a man who has suffered deeply. To find you married to Geoffrey was a terrible blow to him.'

'To his pride – not to his love,' said Pamela. 'He very soon fell in love with *you.*'

Stella caught her breath and looked at her sister. Pamela's tone had savoured of jealousy. That was so like Pam! She always hated anyone to pay more attention to her, Stella, than to herself. She was piqued by the thought that Julian had not broken his heart for her. Strangely selfish! A strange, inconsistent, warped nature was Pam's!

'Pam,' said Stella, quietly, 'you don't love Julian anymore. You have loved Geoffrey. It can't matter to you that Julian loves me.'

'Oh, no!' said Pamela, shrugging her shoulders.

Silence a moment. Then Pamela added:

'But I shall come down to Lyndhurst with you. I must be with you – or go mad.'

Stella immediately softened.

'My poor dear! Yes, I understand. You shall come. But you must stay at the "Crown," and not at Eden Hall. There has already been trouble – with the bedroom question . . .' A burning flush dyed her face and throat, and as Pamela stared at her inquisitively she went on. 'Someone stayed one week-end, and Julian and I were forced into the same room – we had to sit up all night. That mustn't happen again.'

'What a situation!' said Pamela. 'It would be funny if it weren't so serious.'

'It is far from 'funny,'' said Stella.

'Oh, well, I'll put up at the 'Crown,' ' said Pamela. 'And I can spend the day with you.'

'My dear, you'll have to be terribly careful.' Stella warned her. 'Lady Eden's state of health is very precarious, and Julian's one wish in life is to spare her unhappiness. She firmly believes I am Pamela – and she loves me.'

'Continue to be Pamela. I'll be Mrs. Geoffrey Raynes – your sister, Stella,' said Pamela.

Stella rose and began to pace up and down the room.

'I don't like it,' she said in a low tone. 'I don't like it at all. It is all wrong!'

'It's too late to moralise,' said Pamela. 'The tangle will have to unravel itself. I promise not to upset Lady Eden anyhow.'

'Thank heaven for so much!' said Stella.

She sat down on the couch again and put her aching head between her hands.

The next two days were like a nightmare to Stella. First there was Geoffrey's funeral; Pamela, hysterical with grief, leaning on her for support – blind to everything save her torn emotions of the moment. On Stella's back, as usual, fell the burden. She must be comforter, advisor, mother, sister, all in one.

And after poor Geoffrey Raynes had been laid to rest, they had to settle up accounts at the hotel and leave Paris for England.

Stella had written to Julian the previous day, warning him that Pamela was accompanying her to Lyndhurst. She wondered with painful anxiety what he would say and do when he saw his wife again . . . what the consequences of the visit would be.

During the journey home, Pamela remained silent, almost sullen, wrapped in widow's weeds which made her pale little face look paler and younger than ever. She refused to discuss the future at all.

'See what happens – don't try and map out anything,' she said, whenever Stella made an attempt to talk things over.

So Stella was forced to keep silence and was left to her own anxious, troubled thoughts.

About a dozen times she pictured the meeting between Julian and his wife. And every time she saw Julian embarrassed and tongue-tied; Pamela cold and emotionless. What a meeting it would be . . . she, his wife . . . wearing widow's weeds for another man!

The two girls reached Lyndhurst late that night. Stella went straight to the 'Crown Hotel' with Pamela, and saw that she had a comfortable bedroom. Then she telephoned to Eden Hall.

'Is that you, Julian?' she asked, as his familiar voice answered her call.

'Yes . . . oh, my dear, then you are back!' came his answer.

She thrilled as she heard the love-note throb in his voice.

'Yes. Pamela is with me. Julian, how are things? Pamela insists upon coming to Eden Hall with me to-night.'

Silence. Then Julian said:

'I hate the idea of it, but I suppose she must come. I'll induce mother to go to bed early, and you can go up to her and pretend everything is all right.'

'Yes. Very well. We'll dine here in the hotel and be with you about nine o'clock.'

'Very well. Stella, darling . . .'

'Yes, my dear?'

'Do you still love me?'

'Oh, you know it!' she answered, her mouth close to the transmitter, her face aflame.

'Oh, my darling!' he said. 'Good-bye till we meet.'

'Good-bye,' she said.

She hung up the receiver and pressed her hands to her burning cheeks.

'Oh, I love him – I love him!' she said to herself. 'How is all this going to end?'

Pamela was in a curious mood during dinner. She was quiet and thoughtful, and there was a peculiar questioning look in her eyes that perplexed Stella.

'What is she thinking of? What does she mean to say or do when she sees Julian?' she reflected.

There was but one thing to hope; that was that Pamela would quietly arrange the divorce with Julian. It was the only thing that could bring happiness to all three of them.

Stella and Pamela took a taxi from the 'Crown' to Eden Hall. Stella did not know what her sister was feeling, but she, herself, was shaking with nervousness.

Hannah greeted them in the hall. She beamed at Stella.

'Glad to see you safely back, ma'am,' she said.

'Thank you, Hannah,' said Stella, conscious of a guilty blush. 'Where is – the master?'

'In the library, ma'am.'

Stella glanced hurriedly at Pamela; saw that the girl's lips were curved in a curious smile – a smile that was almost a sneer.

Her heart jerked painfully fast. She opened the library

door and half-pushed Pamela inside.

'There,' she said. 'Julian is there!'

Pamela's husband came slowly across the room toward the two girls.

In moments of great embarrassment, where it is difficult to know what to say or do, women are nearly always more self-possessed than men; more capable of hiding confusion under a calm smile.

Julian Eden – faced with the girl he had married on a hot impulse, a year ago, and who had since been married to another man – felt utterly awkward and speechless. He looked at her quickly, almost furtively – then looked away again – cleared his throat – glanced at Stella as though for support.

But Pamela was neither confused nor tongue-tied. With marvellous self-possession she walked to Julian and offered him her hand.

'Well, Julian?' she said.

He took the hand she gave him, remembering its smallness, its whiteness; but dropped it again almost immediately.

'Well, Pamela,' he said in a low, nervous voice.

Stella's heart beat furiously. She could not take her eyes off Julian's face. Every nerve in her body quivered; yearned for him. She had not seen him for several days, and the short separation had proved how much she loved him – how necessary he had become to her life – she wanted to fling herself into his arms and cling to him – feel the passionate pressure of his lips.

But like a slender black shadow, Pamela stood between them; that queer, half-sneering smile still playing about her lips.

'I – I think I'll run upstairs and see your mother, Julian,' said Stella hurriedly.

His blue eyes met and held hers for an instant. She read love and longing in them – a silent plea for forgiveness because he dared not even touch her hand.

Turning, she walked swiftly out of the library, and shut the door behind her.

She walked up the staircase, and then paused on the first landing. Pressing her hands to her eyes for a moment, she made an effort to control the emotions that were fast weakening her.

'I'm tired – therefore hysterical,' she told herself. 'I mustn't give way – for mother's sake . . .'

She must go to Lady Eden in a normal frame of mind; speak and smile naturally; keep that beloved woman from suspecting that anything was wrong. But she was tired – terribly tired and sick at heart. The situation had been difficult to deal with before. Now it was doubly hard. Pamela – Julian's rightful, lawful wife – was here at Eden Hall. Her presence made all the difference. What chance had she, Stella, and Julian, of snatching an hour's happiness – now that Pamela had come back?

She drew a hand across her eyes, then flung back her head.

'I mustn't give way,' she thought. 'I *must* remember that there are others than myself to be considered in this matter!'

With firm, quick footsteps she walked to Lady Eden's bedroom, knocked at the door, then in answer to the soft 'Come in,' entered.

Lady Eden – fragile and pathetic on her great pillows – held out both her hands to the girl.

'My darling,' she said. 'So it is you! I hoped it might be. How I have missed you!'

Tears rushed to Stella's eyes. She went down on one knee beside the bed and laid her head on the old lady's shoulder. Lady Eden circled the slim figure with her arms – patted the bowed, dark head with tender fingers.

'Darling Pamela,' she murmured. 'I can't tell you how Julian and I have missed you! I've been bad enough – but

Julian has been like a lost soul, wandering about the house waiting for his little wife to come home.'

'I have missed you both, too.' Stella spoke in a husky emotional voice – her face still hidden. 'Dearest mother. . . '

'How are you, child?'

'Oh – quite well. A little tired, perhaps.'

'Or course . . . that long journey from Paris . . .'Lady Eden nodded. She went on stroking the girl's soft hair. 'And your sister? Has she borne the journey well?'

'Yes, quite,' answered Stella. 'She is downstairs with Julian.'

'Poor little thing,' said Lady Eden. 'I feel so dreadfully sorry for her. It is tragic – losing her husband on their honeymoon like that.'

'Yes, it is awful,' said Stella.

'You are very devoted to each other, aren't you, dear?' asked the old lady. 'Julian was telling me so.'

'Yes – we have always been – very closely knit,' said Stella, swallowing hard.

'You must be a great comfort to her. You have asked her to stay with us as long as she likes, haven't you?'

'She is – staying in Lyndhurst at the 'Crown,' but not at Eden Hall,' said Stella, trying to speak calmly. 'She thinks it better – she is so anxious not to be in the way.'

'I call that very thoughtful of her,' said Lady Eden. 'She must be a very nice girl . . . because, of course, you and Julian are like honeymooners, and don't want a third constantly with you.'

Stella did not reply. She closed her eyes and set her teeth, trying hard to conquer the feeling of sick misery that threatened to overwhelm her. How she loathed the deception of this innocent, sweet woman; how hard it was to keep still; to listen to all that Lady Eden had to say! It was all so wrong – so futile!

'I'm longing to meet Stella,' she heard Lady Eden

observe. 'If she is anything like you, Pamela – she will soon win my heart.'

'She is – very sweet – but unlike me to look at,' said Stella. 'She is fair and petite.'

'The name Pamela would have suited her; whereas you ought to be Stella,' said Lady Eden with a tranquil smile.

Stella felt an hysterical desire to burst out laughing. If only Julian's mother knew . . . knew that it *was* Pamela downstairs with Julian; Stella beside her bed.

She felt she could bear no more of this. She kissed Lady Eden and rose to her feet.

'I must go and wash and tidy, Mother darling,' she said. 'Are you going to sleep now? Shall I say good night, or come in again?'

'Say good night now, dear,' smiled Lady Eden. 'I daresay you and your sister have much to talk about with Julian. Let me see – isn't it the first time he has seen his sister-in-law?'

'Yes,' Stella forced the word.

'Well, well! . . .I shall see her in the morning. Give her my love.'

They exchanged another kiss; then Stella sought her own bedroom. It was some time before she emerged downstairs again.

The conversation between Julian and Pamela, during Stella's absence, had been somewhat strained.

Left alone with his wife, Julian had politely asked her to sit down, then seated himself opposite her.

'Do you mind if I smoke?' he asked.

'Not at all,' said Pamela.

She stared curiously at him. He had altered very considerably since she had last seen him. Stella was right, she thought; the gay, inconsequent young airman she had married, had vanished – for ever. This man with the stern mouth; the handsome, scarred face; the blue brooding eyes – was the same Julian – yet a total stranger to her. It seemed extraordinary that she should meet him in this cold-blooded way; shake hands with him; sit apart from him; neither of them experience one thrill of emotion – and yet once they had been passionate lovers!

So much had happened in one year that had divided them . . . so much! Pamela's thoughts turned to the quiet, charming, adoring husband whom she had buried in Paris yesterday. She had loved Geoffrey. She was inconsolable for his loss. Real pain smote her heart for a moment, and she looked away from Julian; her small hands clenching in her lap.

But even then her overweening vanity was uppermost; her love for melodrama; of producing effects upon people. Even then – with tragic memories of Geoffrey Raynes at the back of her mind – Pamela wondered what Julian was thinking of her; whether or not he felt compassion for her; she knew how appealing she looked in her widow's weeds. She did not like his calm attitude. It would have pleased her better had he shown emotion at her return. She forgot that he was in love with Stella; chose, perhaps, only to remember that once he had loved her, Pamela.

And he – heaven alone knew the chaos of thought in Julian Eden's mind at that moment. He sat back in his chair, smoking fiercely, trying to get a grip upon himself. He had wanted to follow Stella out of the library – fold her to his heart – kiss her again and again – drink deeply of those sweet lips – look deeply into those grey, dear eyes – tell her how wretched he had been while she had been away. But here he was, sitting opposite his wife . . . *his wife*! was it possible? Of course, the laws were all wrong. It was too absurd to consider that this girl, wearing widow's weeds for another man – this girl who had belonged to Geoffrey Raynes – was still *his* wife! Yet it was so.

Furtively he glanced at her. She was not looking at him, but at her hands; such pretty, useless, butterfly hands – so unlike Stella's strong, capable, tender fingers.

Why had he ever loved and married Pamela? He was

amazed at the passion that had swept him off his feet – led him into a secret marriage with her. He was amazed now – and conscious that her presence only confused him – did not thrill him for a single moment. He had never wanted to see her, or hear her speak, again.

Scrutinising her more closely, he decided that she had not altered physically. She was the same dainty, pink and white and gold Pamela of old days. Her heavy mourning gave her rather a delicate, wan appearance, and the sorrowful expression in the big blue eyes added, perhaps, to the appeal of her beauty. Julian wondered, cynically, if she had really loved Raynes; if her grief for him were enduring – or merely transient – like her grief for him, Julian, had been?

It was hard to tell. Time alone could prove it.

He felt that he must say something. This silence between them was unbearable.

'I feel I would like to – to tell you how sorry I am for all that has happened to you, Pamela,' he said.

She raised her golden head and looked at him.

'Thank you, Julian,' she said. 'But surely you feel no pity for me? You must consider that I deserve my punishment, since I was so quick to – forget you.'

He flushed and frowned.

'I don't think we'd better talk about it, Pamela,' he said.

She leaned forward, clasping her arms about her knees.

'Oh, but we must – we must talk it all out! she said.

Grimly he thought:

'She always loved 'scenes.' I suppose she wants a 'scene' now.'

'Julian,' she said. 'I felt certain you were dead.' – you can be sure I would not have married again had I not been certain.'

'Of course,' he said. 'I was reported 'Believed dead.' You might perhaps have given me a little longer to put in an appearance.'

Pamela bit her lip.

'I was certain,' she muttered. 'And when Geoffrey came along, I – I didn't wait – that's all.'

'Quite so. I believe thousand of women married within a year of their husbands being killed in the War; and so why should you not re-marry after my accident in the 'plane?'

'You are cynical and resentful, of course,' said Pamela, with a deep sigh. 'I know I deserve it.'

'Don't let it worry you now,' said Julian, brutally. 'It is much too late. And in any case it showed us both what a couple of fools we were to have married – to have imagined ourselves in love. It was the folly of extreme youth.'

A slow flush stained Pamela's fair face. Hers was not a nature to like hearing a man admit himself a 'fool' for having loved and married her. It was an immediate challenge to her. She locked her slender fingers and worked them nervously up and down.

'You are very harsh, Julian,' she said in a plaintive voice. 'You have changed very much.'

'I daresay,' he said. 'To come back from the hell from which I returned, and find one's wife married again within a few months, is not likely to make one soft and gentle.'

'Well, you needn't cast all the accusations at me,' said Pamela suddenly. 'It hasn't taken you long to get over *my* loss, Julian!'

He looked at her – his whole body stiffening. He knew then that Stella had told Pamela about their love. His lips tightened.

'You are quite right,' he said quietly. 'I soon got over it.'

'And now we're all in a nice mess,' said Pamela resentfully. 'I don't know what's going to happen.'

Julian rose and began to pace up and down the library. He had finished one cigarette and lit another. Hands thrust in his pockets, he paused before Pamela and stared down at her a moment.

'Look here, Pamela,' he said. 'What has been done, here

at Eden Hall, has been done for my mother's sake. My mother is very precious to me, and her heart is weak. Stella has been helping me deceive her into thinking Stella my wife, and she is perfectly happy. Whatever happens, you must help us keep mother in ignorance of the truth.'

Pamela shrugged her shoulders.

'Oh, I don't want to hurt your mother! Not that she was very kind to me, at one time.'

Julian bit at his lips.

'No – I admit that. The fact that I had married secretly distressed her – and my father. But that is all passed.'

'And are we all to remain permanently in this delightful position?' inquired Pamela, in a sarcastic tone.

'Until some good way out of the tangle presents itself,' he said. 'Pamela, you know that Stella and I love each other, don't you?'

'So she said.'

'And you loved your – the man who has died,' said Julian, stumbling a little over his words. 'You will want to keep faithful to his memory, I know. Therefore, the best thing that can happen is for you and I to – separate entirely.'

Pamela did not answer for a moment. She sat silent, twisting her wedding ring round and round her finger. Julian watched her almost anxiously. What was she thinking? So much depended on her actions. He wondered . . .

'We shall have to all think things over,' at last she said. 'It is no use rushing into any decisions to-night.'

'Quite so,' said Julian.

The library door opened. Stella came into the room.

Soon after Stella had joined them, Pamela departed back to her hotel. She saw no object in remaining at Eden Hall that evening. All three of them were too embarrassed and wretched to attempt frank discussion of the position.

Julian drove his wife back to the 'Crown' in his car. They exchanged very formal 'good nights.' Then Julian returned home and walked straight into the library, conscious of intense desire to see Stella alone.

She was waiting for him; a little pale and heavy-eyed but infinitely beautiful to him.

He took her in his arms without speaking and held her close to him for a long moment. Then he said:

'Oh, my dear . . . how is it all going to end?'

'Heaven knows!' she said sighing. 'It is all too awful, too perplexing for words.'

'I only know one thing,' said Julian savagely. 'That is – the sight of Pamela had made me realise all the more how much I love you, Stella.'

She closed her eyes and leaned her cheek against his.

'My dear, my dear . . .' she whispered.

'I love you,' he repeated. 'Love you so much that I can't – I won't live without you, Stella. While you were in Paris, I felt lost – I wanted you terribly. Now that I have got you back, I can't – I won't let you go.'

His hands held her to him with an intensity that made her catch her breath. She could feel his heart pounding against hers.

'My love . . . my love!' he said. 'I love you – I love you!'

All the passion and longing in her responded to the passion, the longing in him. She wound her arms about his neck. Pamela was forgotten – everything on earth was forgotten except this great white flame of love that wrapped them about; burned them; melted them into one soul.

She gave him her lips, and her eyes shut as she felt his mouth touch hers . . . press deeper . . . bruise them in a kiss that assuaged all the passionate yearning of the past few days.

For a long, long while they stood thus, locked in that embrace. When at last Julian's hold of her relaxed, she felt herself trembling, as though with ague, and weakly she leaned against him. He stroked her hair with one hand, his face white.

'Oh, my dear,' she said, 'we mustn't – we mustn't love each other like this. It – is wrong.'

'Right or wrong, it is divine, Stella,' he said hoarsely. 'If you knew what it is to me to hold you, to kiss you again!'

'I know. Don't you think I feel just like you do?'

'Then, my dear, my dearest – how can we help it?'

'Because we have got to – got to be strong,' she said breathing jerkily. 'We must remember . . . Pamela is in Lyndhurst – she is your wife – I am not.'

'But you shall be!' he said fiercely. 'You shall be – I am determined.'

'Please heaven – one day,' said Stella, hiding her eyes on his shoulder. 'But I am not yet, and we must not give way to our love, Julian.'

He held her closely, in an almost jealous grip.

'Pamela must let me arrange a divorce,' he said. 'She must!'

'I expect she will, Julian.'

'I don't know. I'm afraid.'

'Why afraid?' She looked up at him swiftly.

'I don't trust Pamela. She is a queer girl – she is not open and frank like you, Stella. I don't believe in her – even in her love for Raynes. She is so superficial.'

Stella winced.

'No, no Julian – she is not as bad as that!'

'To please a whim she may refuse to let me divorce her,' said Julian hoarsely. 'She would say nothing definite to-night. She did not seem to wish to discuss it.'

'But she will to-morrow – later, anyhow.'

'If anything happened that I couldn't marry you, Stella, I'd go mad!' he said.

'Hush, darling!' she said. 'Try to be calm – for all our sakes.'

He covered her face with kisses – hair, lips, eyes, cheeks – then her throat. Then gently he put her from him – his eyes blue-black in his haggard face.

'I need to be strong and calm,' he said. 'My love for you is overwhelming me.'

The tears started to her eyes.

'Dearest, I know and understand,' she said.

'You are a saint. You would understand anything,' he said. 'Even what selfish, jealous brutes and beast we men are.'

'There is nothing brutal or beastly in great love, Julian,' she said.

He took her hand and pressed it to his hot eyes.

'I am going to bed, darling,' he said. 'Good night. Perhaps we shall all see more light to-morrow.'

As though fearing to touch her or kiss her or speak again, he went quickly out of the room and left her alone.

She sank on the sofa and buried her face in her hands.

CHAPTER 12

A month went by, bringing no alteration in the situation – no relief from the strain of it.

Pamela remained at the hotel in Lyndhurst and spent all day at Eden Hall. Julian and Stella had grown almost used to the sight of the girl in her black robes, flitting like a slim, dark shadow about the sunlit garden; or sitting with them in the house – eating with them – treated as one of the family.

One grows used to situations, yet one is never at ease, fundamentally. Neither Stella nor Julian felt easy when Pamela was present. They were always on edge; afraid lest she should by word, gesture or look betray to Lady Eden the fact that she was the real Pamela even – Julian's wife.

But Pamela gave no cause for anxiety. She acted her part very nicely and addressed her sister as 'Pam' with a sang-froid that surprised Stella. When Lady Eden was present, she also affected the rôle of sorrowing young widow and completely won the old Lady's sympathy. Lady Eden was genuinely sorry for Pamela. But she did not honestly like her. There was something about her that prevented Lady Eden from becoming fond of her – an unknown something which she was quite unable to explain to herself.

'She is a pathetic, sweet little thing, and yet she has not the frank charm and attraction of my Julian's wife,' Lady Eden told herself again and again.

So the little drama went on.

Julian and Stella sought to come to some definite understanding with Pamela, and found it difficult – almost impossible. Pamela behaved in a curious, baffling manner. She avoided discussion of the past or present. She seemed determined to live only in the moment.

'I feel too unhappy to talk over things yet,' she told her husband on more than one occasion. 'All I want is to remain here as your sister-in-law for the present. Do let things rest.'

But of course Julian chafed against the situation – and Stella shared his anxiety and distress. They were passionate lovers; they longed for each other – for peace, for security in their love. And they were denied these things. They were forced to oscillate perpetually between misery, uncertainty and rapture.

Julian began to find the state of affairs intolerable. Not only were his nerves stretched to breaking-point, but he had begun to hate the sight of his wife; to dread her approaching footsteps. When he was with her, he found her continually staring at him with those great, blue, mournful eyes; and in contradiction to the pathos of the eyes was the semi-sneer on the petulant little mouth.

He begged Stella to come to an understanding with her sister, but Stella found herself up against a brick wall when she approached Pamela.

'I really don't wish to do anything in the matter just yet,' she told Stella with her strange, cool smile. 'I'm happy as I am.'

'Yes, but can't you see that Julian and I are not happy?' Stella said, conscious of a burning flush.

'If it comes to truth I'm not actually *happy*,' said Pamela. 'I never forget my darling Geoffrey. But I am finding peace and comfort at Lyndhurst – and really it is better for things to go on as they are until the old lady dies.'

Stella looked at her sister in despair. She did not understand Pamela. Was it true that she 'never forgot' her darling Geoffrey? Was her grief sincere? Somehow, it did not strike Stella as being either true or lasting. Pamela was no longer pale or torn by emotion. She was self-possessed;

pink-cheeked, smiling again. And Stella had seen her stare at Julian . . . wondered what lay behind those blue, guileless eyes.

Surely Pamela did not mean to attempt a reconciliation between her husband and herself? The idea terrified Stella. She dared not communicate her fears to Julian; yet in a curious, psychic way she knew that Julian felt exactly the same fear.

And none of them spoke their minds aloud. They only thought . . . and looked . . . Stella and Julian haunted by their unspoken anxieties; Pamela watching them, maintaining her stubborn, baffling attitude.

One afternoon of late July, they sat at tea on the lawn just outside the French windows of the dining-room.

Julian sat next to his mother. Pamela and Stella were opposite.

Stella was pouring out tea. Lady Eden was sitting back in her chair, talking to her son – her tranquil face smiling. She, alone of them all, knew peace of mind – contentment – happiness.

'Julian, I'm coming to the conclusion that you are not looking quite so well, dear,' she was saying. 'You aren't feeling the effects of your accident again, are you?'

'No, Mother, thanks,' he said. 'I'm quite all right.'

'What do you think of him, Pamela?' asked Lady Eden, turning to Stella.

'Oh – he – I think he's all right,' stammered the girl.

'Perhaps he's in need of a change,' suggested the old lady. 'Julian, why don't you take your wife to the seaside for a few weeks?'

Julian and Stella exchanged glances. There was bitter yearning – almost despair in that look. Pamela saw it. She looked down at her lap with a queer, secretive little smile.

'I don't need a change, Mother,' said Julian. 'I'd rather not go away. I prefer to stay in Lyndhurst.'

And with that he drained his cup, passed it to Stella for

more, and changed the conversation.

Edith, the parlourmaid, came out of the dining-room. A tall man in a grey lounge suit followed her.

'Please, sir, a friend to see you,' she said to Julian.

'Who is it?' began Julian rising.

Then he paused. His face flushed scarlet and afterwards grew white. He stared with unbelieving eyes at the visitor, who rushed at him, gripping his hand.

'Julian, old fellow! By Jove, I'm glad to see you again. Have I surprised you? Just got home from the West Coast of Africa, and I felt I must look you up.'

Stella watched the meeting between the two men unmoved. But Pamela had risen; Pamela's pretty face was aflame. And the next moment Stella knew the catastrophe that had happened.

The visitor, his good-looking, sunburned face beaming, had turned to Pamela and gripped her hand.

'I'm awfully glad to see you again, *Mrs. Eden,*' He exclaimed. 'It's just about thirteen months ago since I was best man at your wedding, eh? You haven't forgotten me, I hope. You know I went abroad soon after you and Julian were married. How are you? How are you both?'

The silence that followed the stranger's greeting was so profound that Stella felt she could hear the loud beating of her heart. She sat back in her chair, transfixed with dismay and astonishment – staring at the man who was wringing Pamela's hand and addressing her as 'Mrs. Eden.'

Julian's face was as white as death; Pamela's was red. Lady Eden was staring from one to another, her delicate ivory face puckered with perplexity.

The man who had witnessed Julian's wedding became suddenly conscious of the silence and tension, and the fact that nobody spoke to him. He dropped Pamela's hand. Turning to Julian, he looked at him inquiringly.

'Nothing wrong, old chap, is there?'

And then he looked back at Pamela and saw her widow's

weeds. It was his turn to show astonishment. His sunburned face wrinkled up. He stood there, rather nervously, at a loss for words. Lady Eden was the first to speak.

'Isn't there some mistake?' she said gently. 'The lady you have just spoken to is Mrs. Raynes. This is my son's wife – Mrs. Eden. . . .'

She indicated Stella, who looked at Julian with terrified eyes.

Julian acted promptly.

'Mother – let me introduce you to Major Lucas, who was in France with me during the War,' he said in a quick, nervous voice. 'He was also my best man at my wedding. But he's forgotten Pam just for the moment – haven't you, Arthur? . . . ' He put a hand on Major Lucas's arm, and went on talking, without giving the bewildered man time to argue. 'That's Pam – my wife – in the chair – in the white tennis frock. She's dark. I can't think how you came to make such a mistake. Stella, my sister-in-law, is quite fair. How are you, Arthur, old fellow? Delighted to see you again. Just come home on leave from the West Coast, eh?'

He rattled on – conscious that he was literally fighting for life – his mother's life. His cheerful voice relieved the tension and restored Stella's calm. Lady Eden still looked utterly astonished but – Stella reflected with enormous relief – unsuspicious.

Major Lucas was speaking now.

'But, my dear Julian, I remember Pamela and –'

'I'm going to take you indoors to my study for a chat, Arthur,' Julian broke in hurriedly. 'It's a long time since we met . . . Come along.'

He started to pull Lucas toward the house. Lady Eden called after him.

'But Julian dear, tea is just coming, and I'm sure Major Lucas would like some tea.'

'All right, Mother, we'll come back in a second,' said Julian, avoiding his mother's innocent eyes. 'Just a few moments in my study – one cigarette.'

The two men disappeared.

Stella breathed again. She was still feeling cold with fear, but she knew that the worst moment had passed. Julian had managed to get Major Lucas away, and now, of course, he would explain matters. It had been a narrow shave . . . never had Lady Eden been nearer discovery of the truth. But the catastrophe had been averted – for the time being, anyhow.

Pamela had sat down again, a peculiar little smile twisting her lips. She cast a sly glance at Stella. The latter cleared her throat and looked at Lady Eden. She felt it necessary to make some remark.

'How stupid of Major Lucas to have forgotten me!' she stammered.

'Most extraordinary!' exclaimed Lady Eden. 'I can't understand such a thing happening. He was Julian's best man at the wedding, and must have known you quite well, Pamela?'

'Not so v-very well,' said Stella, flushing crimson. 'I only met him once or twice before my wedding.'

'Even then, how could he mistake Stella for you?' persisted Lady Eden. 'You have dark hair – Stella's is golden.'

The girl who wore mourning for Geoffrey Raynes continued to smile that queer twisted little smile. The situation amused her greatly at times. She thought it extraordinarily funny that she should be sitting here, spoken of as 'Stella,' while the real Stella was looked upon as Julian's wife. Of course, she knew Arthur Lucas quite well; a great friend of Julian's in the old days; rather a heavy, phlegmatic individual, but honest and nice, and quite well-off. What must he be thinking of all this? She wondered if he were in Julian's study, hearing the whole strange story, and what he would do when he had heard it?

'I – I fancy Major Lucas's head was injured during the War,' Stella was saying to Lady Eden. 'He always had lapses of memory and the facility for mixing people up. That accounts for it, Mother.'

'Ah – perhaps so,' nodded Lady Eden.

Stella thought:

'Another lie. There is nothing wrong with his head, so far as I know. How many more lies will I have to tell before I have finished?'

Her beautiful grey eyes looked anxiously toward the window of Julian's study. What was going on in there? Would Julian be able to silence his friend? Perhaps Arthur Lucas was a man of high principles – a man who might consider it a sin to countenance the deception. If so – what then?'

Stella moved restlessly on her chair and sighed.

She wondered how much longer she would be called upon to bear the strain of playing this part. She could see nothing but trouble ahead. Each day they seemed to get further and further away from the peace and happiness they craved – all of them.

In Julian's study, the two men were facing each other; Julian worried, ill-at-ease; Lucas still in a state of bewilderment. Julian offered the other man a cigarette.

'Sit down, Arthur,' he said.

'Thanks, I'd rather stand,' said Lucas.

He leaned against the mantelpiece and stared down at Julian, who seated himself. Arthur Lucas was a few years older than Julian and of totally different temperament. During the War a friendship had sprung up between the two, as so often happens with people who are opposites. Lucas – stolid, good-natured, idealistic – had found the younger man an amusing, brilliant companion; and Julian had often gone to Arthur – then his senior officer – for advice over Army and personal affairs.

The major had not approved of the secret marriage between his friend and Pamela Morris – the pretty, golden haired typist. He had done his best to dissuade Julian from, making the match; also he had impressed it upon Julian that the correct thing to do was to inform his parents of the affair.

Julian, at that period of his life, headstrong and inconsequent, had not listened to reason or good counsel. He had rushed into the marriage and decided to keep it a secret until he returned from his world-flight. Lucas then left the Army and had gone abroad, having acted as best man at the wedding which he did not approve, simply and solely out of affection for the younger man.

Now, back in England, Lucas had come with all haste to see Julian. He had heard, in Africa, of the accident and supposed death of his friend, and later of his miraculous restoration to his family. When he had come into the garden of Eden Hall and seen Pamela sitting there beside Julian, he had felt only relief and delight, believing that the marriage was no longer a secret, and that Pamela had been taken into the family by her mother-in-law, and that all was well.

His surprise and perplexity can be imagined when Julian had denied that the golden-haired girl, whom Lucas well remembered, was his wife.

'Now, Julian, old fellow, for heaven's sake, what's all this mystery?' he said. 'Why is Pamela in widow's weeds, and why are you calling that dark-haired girl your wife?'

Julian smoked fiercely for a moment. Then he said in a low tone:

'You don't think you've made a mistake, Arthur? . . . that your memory has led you astray?'

'Good gracious me, no!' said Lucas, running his fingers through his thick fair hair which was slightly streaked with grey. 'I remembered your bride, my dear fellow. Does a 'best man' forget? Come – what's the mystery? I'm amazed!'

Julian shrugged his shoulders in a hopeless sort of way.

'I suppose I must tell you, Arthur.'

'Not if you don't wish to,' said Lucas.

'I'm only too glad to confide in you, Arthur,' said Julian, looking up at his friend with a sudden, warm affection in his eyes. 'It's like the good old times. But God knows, I wish I hadn't to tell you *this* story. It's a sorry tale.'

'Go ahead, old chap,' said Lucas, puffing quietly at his cigarette.

So Julian told him – everything. Major Lucas listened, his placid face becoming more and more puckered with astonishment and anxiety every moment.

'So you see what a ghastly mess we're all in,' Julian finished. 'We dare not let my mother know the truth, and Stella and I are madly, desperately in love with each other.'

'Good Lord! What a position!' said Lucas, his voice aghast.

He stared down at Julian, who was sitting in an attitude of despair, his head between his hands.

'My dear chap,' he added. 'It's the most amazing tale I've ever listened to. I can scarcely believe it. One reads of these things – sees them on the films – but one doesn't expect to come up against them in the lives of one's own friends.'

'No – you're right,' said Julian, bitterly. 'Imagine what I felt when I got back to find Pamela married again and her sister living here as my widow!'

'I think it was outrageous!' said Lucas, his suntanned face reddening. 'Outrageous of Stella to come here in that guise. She is to blame for the whole unfortunate affair.'

'No, Arthur,' said Julian quickly, 'don't be hard on Stella. She's the most wonderful girl on earth, if you but knew it.'

'You are infatuated with her,' said Lucas, impatiently. 'Really, Julian, I'm surprised at you! How can you fall in love with a girl who has brought so much trouble upon you all – and your own wife's sister, too!'

It was Julian's turn to flush. He tapped one clenched fist on the arm of his chair.

'You'll never understand, Lucas,' he said. 'You aren't my nature. You're the sort of stolid chap that never loses his head or his heart – that's why you're still a batchelor. I'm not going to say I lose my heart to every pretty woman I meet. I don't. I had a boyish infatuation for Pamela. But I *love* Stella. She is my real mate – I know it –' he broke off, the muscles in his throat working, his handsome face scarlet and embarrassed.

Major Lucas looked at him pityingly.

'My dear chap, I'm damned sorry for you,' he said, 'if you feel like that! But whether Stella Morris is the angel you think her, or the adventuress she appears to have been, it's all the same in the end. You've got to fight your feelings like the very deuce, and remember that Pamela is your wife.'

'Pamela is Geoffrey Raynes' widow,' said Julian, hotly. 'Why should I feel any responsibility – any loyalty towards the girl who forgot my existence within twelve months?'

'It was rotten of her to marry again so soon, I admit,' said Lucas, his brows knit. 'But all the same, she is still your wife. She never had been Raynes' wife.'

'If Raynes hadn't been killed in that accident, things would have penned out differently,' muttered Julian. 'I might have got a divorce – married Stella. Now, what the dickens am I to do? Pamela is living down here in Lyndhurst – refusing to leave Stella's side, and to make up her mind what she's going to do in the future. She's rich – she's got all Raynes' money. Why shouldn't she let me get a divorce on the grounds that she refuses to live with me – or vice-versa? My mother need never know – I could make Stella my wife, then.'

'Julian, old fellow, you don't seem to see that the whole thing is wrong – unprincipled!' said Lucas.

'Oh, you were always full of ideals and principles! I never was,' said Julian, biting savagely at his lips.

Lucas put a hand on his shoulder.

'You must face the guns and do the right thing, Julian, he said gravely. 'I don't see how you can desert Pamela now that she is alone in the world. She is such a child, and she looks so fragile.'

'Oh, yes, she wins any man's sympathy,' said Julian, with a hard laugh. 'And what about my poor Stella, who has striven so bravely to keep the truth from my mother? *That's* the main point in this business, Arthur. We dare not let my mother guess that Pamela is my wife. You must acknowledge your mistake, out in the garden – for her sake.'

'I don't like it at all.'

'But you'll do it – for her sake – for the sake of our friendship, Arthur. . . .'

Julian stood up and faced his friend, his blue eyes miserable and anxious.

'I adore my mother, Arthur,' he added. 'I don't want her to suffer. She won't live long, I know. Until she dies, I want her to be happy.'

'I understand that,' said the Major. 'My own mother means a great deal to me.'

'Then help me out by keeping quiet,' Julian begged him.

Lucas shook his head in a worried way.

'I hate the whole thing,' he said.

'No more than I hate it,' said Julian, between his teeth.

'It can't go on,' said the Major. 'Lord! It's an awful business!'

'I must see Pamela alone to-morrow and try to come to some definite understanding with her,' said Julian, lighting a fresh cigarette. 'If she's willing – we can fix up the divorce all right, and keep the whole thing quiet from mother.'

'If she's willing, I don't see why it shouldn't be arranged – no,' said Lucas, thoughtfully.

'Come out and have some tea and try not to feel too embarrassed, old fellow,' said Julian, taking his arm. 'Tell me, are you in the Forest for long?'

'I intended putting up at the 'Crown' for a week.'

'Pamela is staying there,' said Julian.

'Then I'd better go,' muttered Lucas.

'No – for heaven's sake, stay. I may need your assistance in some way. You were always a rock, Arthur,' said Julian, with a short, tired laugh.

'Oh, I'll stay if I can be of any help, but seems to me you're all in a devil of a mess,' said Lucas, frankly.

The two returned to the garden.

Lady Eden greeted them with a pleased smile.

'Found out your mistake, Major Lucas?' she murmured.

'Oh – ah! – yes, of course,' stammered Lucas. 'Most foolish of me, Lady Eden. I've no memory for faces – fearful fool at remembering people. Mrs. Raynes must forgive me.'

Stella felt fresh waves of relief surge over her. She caught Julian's eye and smiled. He smiled back at her reassuringly. She knew then that Lucas was 'in the know' and would not give them away.

Nobody noticed the look of cold fury that passed over Pamela's pretty face as she heard Major Lucas calmly correct his supposed 'error.' Nobody guessed the schemes that were forming at the back of her brain; and least of all did Julian himself realise that his wife – changeable, superficial in her emotions as she was – had become attracted by her own husband again, and had definitely decided to win him back.

Arthur Lucas stayed for dinner with the Edens. He did not wish to. He felt horribly uncomfortable the whole time. But he could not very well refuse Lady Eden's kind invitation, so he remained for the evening meal.

When he left, Pamela went with him.

'It will be nice to have an old friend of my brother-in-law's at the hotel with me.' She said, sweetly. 'I've felt rather lonely there at times.'

Lucas regarded her with compassion. She was so pretty and pale and fair in her heavy mourning robes. He could not but feel sorry for her – the common attitude of the male toward an attractive, pathetic member of the opposite sex.

'Poor little thing,' he thought. 'I expect she has had a rotten time.'

Julian heard his wife's speech, and saw Lucas's expression of sympathy. It made him peculiarly angry.

'What does Pamela want to try to get round Arthur for?' he thought. 'She hasn't been lonely at all! She's been at Eden Hall all day since her return.'

It was her way to try to 'get round' any man. She was a born coquette. Her 'deep grief' for Geoffrey had not lasted long.

Julian felt thoroughly moody and depressed that night. He turned thankfully to Stella when at last they were alone in the drawing-room.

'Oh, Julian, how much longer are we going on like this?' she asked in a low, intensely weary voice.

All his passionate love for her leaped to the fore. Arthur's ideals and principles were forgotten. He sat down beside her and took her slim figure into his arms, holding her close to his heart.

'My darling! My darling! he said. 'How long *is* it going on? I don't know. I only know that I can't stand much more of it – and you can't. Pamela seems to be the only one who doesn't feel things badly.'

'She is callous – such a strange little thing,' sighed Stella.

'She doesn't know what love is,' muttered Julian. 'Already her love for poor Raynes is on the wane. I know it.'

Stella put her arms about his neck and laid her dark head on his shoulder. She drew him closer to her with a little hungry gesture.

'Julian, I love you so!' she said, brokenly.

'I love you,' he said. 'My dearest, we *must* do something – and at once. I can't live without you any longer.'

For a single moment longer she abandoned herself to his

passionate kisses, clinging to him. Then she fought him back, her beautiful face strained and pale.

'No, darling – no more,' she said. 'You must let me go. Julian – we mustn't be utterly mad!'

Sanity returned to him. He let her go, and sat apart from her – rolling a cigarette in his shaking fingers. She patted her hair into order, looking at him with sorrowful, tender eyes.

'My poor Julian,' she said.

He bent forward and touched her hair with his lips.

'I'm going to think of some way out of this,' he said. 'To-morrow I shall see Pamela alone – tell her she must divorce me – set me free, so that you and I can marry.'

Stella pressed her hands to her breast.

'Oh, if only she would! But I daren't think what she will say. She has been so queer, so reticent –'

'To-morrow must decide,' said Julian. 'I'm not going on like this any longer.'

The following day was the first of August.

A brilliant sun was shining over the New Forest when Pamela arrived at Eden Hall, after breakfast. Her pretty face wore a little smile of satisfaction. She had had a very pleasant morning meal, in company with Major Lucas. She had quite won the heart of the 'best man' who had attended her wedding; she had suggested that she had always cared for Julian; that she had been swept off her feet by Geoffrey Raynes; but that now she was normal, herself again, and she wanted earnestly to start life over again with her husband.

That had appealed to Lucas. He had thought it the correct thing and told her so.

'The poor little woman,' he had reflected as he listened to Pamela's sad, soft voice. 'She isn't nearly so frivolous as I thought she was. She has quite a good heart. I hope she and Julian patch things up. It will serve Miss Stella Morris right.'

He had no sympathy with Stella whatever. He looked upon her as a designing woman.

So Pamela, having won Major Lucas on her side, smiled as she entered the sunlit garden of Eden Hall this morning.

Stella was usually at the gate about this hour to meet her sister. This morning it was Julian's tall figure standing by the lilac bushes, gravely waiting. His face was set – haggard.

'I want to talk to tou before you join mother and Stella,' he said, abruptly. 'Do you mind coming with me to the summer-house in the rosery? We can be quiet there.'

'Why, yes, Julian,' said Pamela.

She followed him along the narrow gravel-path under the fragrant arch of white and pink roses. When they reached the cool shade of the arbour she sat down, still smiling in a sad, secretive way.

'Now, Pamela,' he said, in a low tone, 'we've got to face facts. You've been down in Lyndhurst some weeks now, and we all know exactly what the other is feeling. We all know, anyhow, that the position has become intolerable and that we must make an effort to relieve it.'

'H'm!' said Pamela, reflectively. 'How can that be done? And why do you suppose that we all know each other's feelings?'

'It is plain to you that Stella and I are in love with one another, isn't it?' said Julian curtly.

The girl's eyes narrowed ever so little.

'I try not to see that,' she said primly.

Julian – quick-tempered – flared up at once.

'What do you mean – you try not to see it?'

'Well, it isn't very nice for me, your wife, to see you, my husband, making love to my sister,' said Pamela, unexpectedly.

Julian stared at her – genuinely astonished.

'But – but I don't see how that affects you, Pamela. You – you ceased to care a rap for me months ago.'

'Did I?'

'You married Raynes. You were wildly in love with him.'

The girl's small white hands quivered in her lap just a little.

'Yes. I know. I thought you were dead when I married Geoff. Had you been alive – to me – I'd never have dreamed of running away from you.'

'Never-the-less you loved Raynes and went to Paris with him, and you told Stella you had never really cared for me.'

Pamela fixed her big blue eyes on her husband. She thought in that moment how attractive his lean brown face had become; how much more attractive the man was than the boy had been in the past.

'Julian, it is possible, surely, that old affections and memories can be revived,' she said, gently.

He went scarlet.

'Oh, you're talking absolute rot!' he protested.

'You are very hard on me, Julian,' Pamela continued in that same soft, pathetic voice. 'But all the weeks I've been here, I've been seeing my mistake in ever thinking I ever cared for any man but you – my husband!'

Julian felt his brow wet. His heart jerked savagely.

'Do you realise what you are saying and doing?' he asked in a violent undertone. 'You are trying to tell me that you want a reconciliation!'

'I do,' she said, suddenly reaching out a hand to him. 'Julian – my husband – you *are* my husband still –' her voice broke. 'Don't think of my other marriage – think only of the days when we loved each other so passionately – and became man and wife! You think you care for Stella – but you can never marry her – never. I shall never release you. You are my husband and I want you to take me back. Julian – Julian – say you will!'

'My dear Pamela,' said Julian, when he could find speech, 'you must be quite mad.'

She looked at him indignantly – her big blue eyes swimming with tears.

'Don't be so unkind, Julian! I am not mad. I am quite sane. Why shouldn't I want to become reconciled with you?'

'Why should you?' he asked brusquely. 'You have never had any real affection for me, Pamela. You very soon forgot me – very soon married again. It is too absurd for words that you should change your mind again so quickly and decide that you wish to – to go back to our old relationship. . . .'

He broke off, his face reddening, his hands clenching and unclenching. He felt thoroughly embarrassed and at the same time angry – angry with this girl who so lightly played with human emotions – who swept everything, but her own selfish desires and fancies aside. He could not feel pity for her. He could not feel in the least flattered by her supposed return of affection. He did not believe in her. Besides, he loved Stella with all his heart and soul, and he was on the verge of hating his wife – hating her because she stood between him and Stella and seemed desirous of permanently separating them.

'Julian – don't be cruel!' he heard Pamela say in a wailing little voice. 'I'm so unhappy.'

'I am sorry,' he said. 'I don't want you to be unhappy. But if you are – you have brought it on yourself.'

'Julian – you cared for me terribly once.'

'Perhaps,' he said grimly. 'But you, yourself, altered my feelings, and I'm afraid I cannot revive dead passions.'

Pamela's fair face burned. She buried her eyes on her arm – her slim body shaking with sobs.

'Oh, you are cruel – cruel!' she moaned.

Julian twisted his head with a movement of exasperation.

'Pamela, for heaven's sake stop crying and talk to me rationally and sensibly!' he exclaimed. 'There can be no question of renewing the old relationship. It is absolutely impossible, now that you have been married to Raynes, and I love Stella. For God's sake pull yourself together!'

He spoke harshly – without an ounce of sympathy in his

voice. It had the desired effect upon Pamela. She realised that it was not the slightest use trying to win her way by using woman's effectual weapon – tears. She wiped her eyes and sat up, her small mouth sullenly compressed.

Julian gave a sigh of relief.

'Now, my dear girl,' for heaven's sake let us discuss the situation with common sense. Really, I am amazed at you, Pamela! You are still in mourning for Geoffrey Raynes, whom Stella avows you loved devotedly – yet you attempt to become reconciled with me! I can't understand it.'

Pamela shrugged her shoulders. Her cheeks were red, and this time the flush was of anger. She had wanted to win Julian back. But she had failed; and with one of her swift, abnormal changes of mood, she felt now that she disliked him – she wanted to hurt him because he had snubbed and slighted her. She did not like being reminded of Geoffrey. Shallow and selfish though she was, she possessed a small conscience, and at times that conscience was troubled by memories of the kind, gentle, adoring husband whom she had deceived, and who had died, believing in her.

'Well,' she said, in a sulky voice, 'if you won't become reconciled – what are we going to do?'

'That's exactly what I wish you to help me to decide,' said Julian.

'I've nothing to say,' snapped Pamela. 'I consider the whole thing is wrong. I am your wife by law, and the right thing to do is for you to take me back.'

'I don't agree,' said Julian, lighting a cigarette and pitching the match out on the gravel path in front of the arbour. His dark brows were drawn together in a frown. 'You don't love me, Pamela, and I don't love you. We would never be happy together.'

'*You* say I don't love you. I didn't say it,' said Pamela.

'You know you do not,' said Julian. 'You don't know what love is, my dear girl. You are as likely to fall in love with Major Lucas as not – with any man who attracts you for the moment. You can't exist without being in love with someone.'

Home-truths are never pleasant, and Pamela did not like having them thrust at her. She gritted her small teeth.

'So that's what you think – is it?' she asked passionately. 'You brute! Just because men like me – that's what you think!'

Julian closed his eyes and opened them again wearily. This was developing into a sordid row, and he hated it. It must stop at once, he mentally decided.

'Now look here, Pamela,' he said abruptly. 'I'm not going to quarrel with you. Once and for all – it is impossible for you ever to live with me as my wife again, after what has happened. So we must make arrangements to separate.'

'Yes,' she said, her nostrils quivering, 'I understand it all. You want to get rid of me – so that you can marry Stella!'

Julian flushed to the roots of his hair.

'You are quite right,' he said icily. 'I do wish to marry Stella. But as far as 'getting rid of you' is concerned – that is rubbish. You got rid of me, so to speak. You married Raynes. I consider you in the light of his widow – not my wife – whatever the law likes to say.'

Pamela sprang to her feet.

'Consider what you like – I am your wife and I refuse to agree to a divorce,' she flashed.

Julian also rose. He was as pale now as he had been red.

'You are going to be spiteful,' he said. 'Just because Stella and I care for each other.'

'You had no right to fall in love,' said Pamela, her hands clenched at her sides. She was beside herself with fury – the fury of a 'woman scorned.' 'My husband and my sister – oh – a pretty pair!' she broke off with a trembling laugh.

'Obviously it is no use talking to you,' said Julian. 'You are not yourself.'

'Oh yes I am! But I'm going to find Stella and tell her what I think of her, and my fine husband who wants to just chuck me aside at the first opportunity,' said Pamela.

She began to half-walk, half-run down the garden path toward the house where she knew she would find her sister. Julian followed her – his lips tightly pressed together. He was not going to let Pamela hurt Stella. If there was to be another scene, then he would be there to defend and protect his loved one.

Stella was alone in the cool drawing-room, arranging flowers. She had gathered some fresh roses, and was filling a big silver bowl that stood on a lacquered table with the fragrant pink and crimson blossoms.

She saw Pamela running towards her followed by Julian, and divined at once that the interview between husband and wife had not been a very pleasant or successful one. Pamela's pretty face was red, blotched with weeping; Julian's brow was stormy.

Stella's heart sank. She put down the roses she had been holding, and held out her hand to her sister.

'Oh, Pam, Pam, what has happened?' she asked.

Pamela ignored the hand. She stood before Stella, looking at her with spiteful, resentful eyes. 'Thanks to you, I'm the most miserable girl in the world!' she began.

'Thanks to me?' repeated Stella, dismayed.

'But why –?'

'I've been doing my level best to make things up with Julian – to become reconciled to him, and he has only been objectionable and horrible,' said Pamela in a passionate voice. 'And it's all thanks to you. Isn't he supposed to be in love with you? What right had you to make him fall in love with you – to carry on with him?'

'Pam!' exclaimed Stella, her beautiful face flushing.

Stella don't let anything Pamela says upset you,' intervened Julian, who had now joined the two girls. 'She is beside herself – she is not responsible for what she says.'

'Yes, I am!' snorted Pamela. 'I say what I mean. You

have robbed me of any chance of being happy with my husband.'

Stella stared at her sister. She wondered if the grief of Geoffrey's accident and death had affected Pamela's brain – if the girl were not really insane? Only a month ago she had been tumultuously sobbing out her sorrow and despair over the loss of Geoffrey. She had said she never wanted to see Julian again. And here, to-day, she declared her desire to 'become reconciled' with her first husband; blamed her, Stella, because Julian had refused to take her back as his wife.

'My dear Pam!' Stella said in a quiet voice. 'Sit down and control yourself. You don't know what you're saying.'

'I do – I do!' said Pamela, shaking from head to foot. 'I'm wretched and lonely, and – I am willing to go back to the old love if Julian is willing. But he is not – it is you who have stolen his love – taken my place in this house.'

Stella, utterly at a loss for words, stared at Julian, who stared back at her, feeling equally helpless. Who could pretend to understand or deal with Pamela? She possessed a queer, warped nature – strange ideas of love and life.

One thing alone was plain to Stella; Pamela would never agree to a divorce. That meant Julian would never be free. Their love could never materialise – never be satisfied. They would have to part. Stella felt sick and wretched. She turned from her lover to the girl who was making everything so difficult.

'Pam,' she said in a shaking voice, 'do you realise what you are doing by refusing to give Julian his freedom?'

'Preventing you from having him – yes.'

Stella flushed and winced.

'Not only that, Pamela. But you are condemning us all to misery. There is Lady Eden to think of – her state of health grows more precarious every day. She is very, very frail. A shock now would certainly end her life – and it is a life that is extremely precious to Julian – and to me.'

'I don't see why Lady Eden should be considered before anyone else,' began Pamela. Julian interrupted her – his blue eyes hard as stones.

'Well, I do. And I say she *shall* be considered!'

Pamela shrugged her shoulders.

'Oh, very well. Let her go on thinking Stella your wife. But as soon as she dies – there will be no need to continue with the deception.'

'That is quite true,' said Stella.

Julian smothered something very like an oath. His wife's attitude maddened him.

Pamela looked at him with a malicious little twist of her lips.

'We can't get much further than that – this morning,' she said. 'But understand, Julian – when you are no longer forced to keep Stella here as your wife – I shall expect you to take me back.'

'You can expect!' said Julian brutally.

Pamela's eyes narrowed.

'I don't think your friend, Major Lucas, would agree with you on this point,' she said.

'Lucas! Oh have you been talking to him up at the 'Crown,' have you?' muttered Julian.

'Yes, I have, and he thinks it is your duty to take me back,' said Pamela.

'We are all sorry for you, darling,' said Stella, gently. 'Your position is by no means an enviable one. But then – we are all in a ghastly position, and I feel it to be my fault for ever having come down to Eden Hall as Julian's wife. Yes, I am very much to blame – I know it,' she finished, her voice thick with tears. Pamela looked at her sullenly. But Julian flung back his head.

'No! I won't have you blame yourself, Stella,' he said. 'You thought I was dead. You came for my mother's sake, and if I'd never returned – this trouble would never have been.

Stella clasped her hands together.

'What are we all going to do?' she said in an agitated voice.

'God knows!' muttered Julian.

'Things will have to stand as they are – for the present,' said Pamela. 'But I'm not going to agree to a divorce. I don't see why I should be deserted by you both – so there!'

She tilted her head and marched out of the room. At the door she swung round.

'I'm going back to the hotel,' she said. 'I know I'm not wanted here. But Major Lucas likes me – he has been very kind and sympathetic. I shall go and talk to him.'

She walked from the room and slammed the door.

Julian and Stella exchanged glances.

'Really – she is like a child,' said Julian. 'She hasn't the common sense or discretion of a grown woman. I don't know what to make of her.'

'She is terribly young and terribly selfish,' said Stella, with a deep sigh. 'At any rate, this makes things hopeless for us, Julian. I deserve it. It is only just.'

'You are not to say that,' he said roughly. He came up to her – swung her into his arms and held her close to his breast for a moment. 'I love you, dearest,' he added passionately. 'I won't allow you to condemn your own actions.'

'Which you, yourself, condemned so bitterly when first you came home,' she reminded him, her eyes full of hot tears.

'I didn't realise that you started the whole deception out of pure love for my mother,' he said. 'But I know it now. Stella, beloved – I swear I shall make you mine – somehow – some day.'

She shook her dark head hopelessly.

'Oh, I don't know – I don't know,' she cried. She buried her face on his shoulder, weeping silently.

CHAPTER 13

Arthur Lucas had always considered himself proof against feminine wiles and charms, yet he found himself decidedly attracted by Julian's young wife.

Pamela was undeniably pretty; added to which she had that fair, frail appearance, that soft, appealing sort of voice, which are always attractive to strong men. The Major found the pretty young face and soft sad voice irresistible.

She spent the rest of the morning talking to him; and by lunch-time he was entirely on her side; he considered Julian had been a brute to the poor little woman, and he was intensely sorry for her. After all, it was not her fault. She had imagined her husband dead – had not committed a crime in marrying again. And now, if she desired to be reconciled to Julian, it was only right. Julian was in the wrong – and Stella, too. Major Lucas was sure that Stella was a scheming woman. She had obviously planned to become the mistress of Eden Hall. She ought to go straight away and leave Julian and Pamela alone – give them a chance of renewing the old affection.

Of course, there was Lady Eden – Lucas was worried about her. He did not want the poor old lady to die of shock or anything of that kind. But whatever happened – whatever he felt – he was deuced sorry for poor little Pamela. He felt quite sentimental as he remembered the day when he had stood at Julian's side – witnessed his marriage to Pamela – over a year ago.

At that time he had disapproved of the match and of

Julian's secrecy about it. He still thought the latter had been wrong; counted it the original cause of all this present distress; but at the same time he understood now what had made Julian fall in love with Pamela. There was something charming and wistful about her that any man would love.

During lunch, which Major Lucas took with Pamela at the hotel, he found himself looking at her often – and once he pulled himself up with a shock;

'It's no good me getting sentimental about her,' he reflected grimly. 'I mustn't be such a fool.'

'But sorry for her . . . yes . . . he was sorry . . . she was so pathetic and lonely . . . she seemed so bitterly distressed by Julian's curt dismissal of her.

Pamela – quite conscious of the effect she had made on Arthur Lucas – smiled to herself. It was very wise to have at least one good string to her bow. She knew that.

Meanwhile she did not intend to let Julian go unpunished. She decided to return to Eden Hall after lunch. Why should she leave Julian and Stella un-molested – allow them to make love to each other – go their own sweet way. No! She was Julian's wife and she was going to make him know it.

Lucas did not accompany her to his friend's house.

'I'm not in the mood to meet either Julian or Stella,' he told Pamela. 'I feel too annoyed about the whole affair. Just give Lady Eden my respects and say I will call tomorrow,' he added awkwardly.

'Very well, I will. And thank you *ever* so much for being so kind to me,' murmured Pamela.

She held out her hand and he took it, marvelling at its diminutive size – its softness. Her big, limpid blue eyes were full of sorrow, of appeal. The Major felt his face grow hot. He pressed the little hand, then dropped it – twisted his fair moustache fiercely as he turned away.

'Poor little woman,' he thought, for the hundredth time.

He looked after her, his brows contracted. His equilibrium was upset. His particularly strong sense of right and wrong was temporarily undermined by that strongest of all things – sex-attraction. Pamela, as a woman, appealed to him. Without any real reason, he blamed Julian and Stella, and absolved Pamela from guilt, over the whole unfortunate affair.

Pamela strolled to Eden Hall in a more contented frame of mind than she had left it in the morning. She had won Arthur Lucas – entirely. That was satisfactory. And now to punish Julian and Stella. She would be constantly with them – without letting Lady Eden guess the fact.

Julian and Stella were by no means contented. They were both terribly worried. And when they saw Pamela they felt fresh anxiety. That little half-smile that played about her mouth betokened no good. What did she intend to do now? they wondered.

Pamela strolled on to the lawn where Lady Eden lay in her invalid's chair – Julian and Stella on either side.

Lady Eden greeted the girl she believed to be Julian's sister-in-law quite kindly, although she had not taken a very great fancy to her.

'Well, my dear,' she murmured. 'How are you?'

'Quite fit, thank you, Lady Eden,' smiled Pamela, seating herself. 'How are you?'

'Oh – so-so!' said the old lady smiling.

'Mother is not quite so well this afternoon, as a matter of fact,' said Julian, with a warning glance at his wife. 'We want to keep her very quiet.'

'I see,' said Pamela, nodding.

'Come for a walk with me, dear,' suggested Stella hurriedly.

'No thanks. I'm tired. I'd like to sit here, if Lady Eden does not mind,' said Pamela.

'Not a bit, my dear,' said the old lady.

Stella bit her lip. She knew that Pamela purposely avoided a tête-à-tête. It was a pity. She had so wanted to talk things over with Pam again – reason with her quietly.

The four of them sat there in silence for a while. Julian was smoking – obviously ill at ease. Stella looked at him, then at Lady Eden's delicate, peaceful face. Poor Julian, she thought, her heart full of tender pity for him. He was so terribly anxious lest anything should happen to bring a cloud across that beloved old face.

'She broke the somewhat strained silence.

'I can't sit here and be idle,' she said, with a little forced laugh. 'I think I'll go out for a walk, even if you won't come – Stella.'

How she hated calling Pam, 'Stella'!

'Do, dear,' said Pamela sweetly, keeping her seat.

Julian wanted to go with Stella. But he dared not. He felt unable to leave his mother alone with Pamela. He did not trust his wife. Miserably he looked up at the girl he loved.

'I'm rather lazy, darling,' he lied. 'I'll stay here, too.'

'I won't be long,' said Stella. 'Just a stroll to the forest. I'll be back before tea-time.'

Pamela saw the long, ardent look exchanged between her husband and sister. It roused all her former jealousy and anger. She tapped her foot on the grass, her eyes narrowing.

After Stella had gone, the three who remained on the lawn were quiet. Julian found it impossible to enter into any conversation with his wife, and Lady Eden's eyes had closed. She seemed to be dozing.

Julian, sure that his mother slept, rose and walked quietly through the French windows into the library. Pamela followed him with her gaze, saw him choose a book, light a pipe, and sit down in an arm-chair.

'So he thinks he can neglect me entirely,' she thought angrily. 'Well, I won't have that!'

She walked into the library and with a cool impudence that took Julian's breath away, seated herself on the arm of his chair.

'What's your book, Julie?' she asked.

'Oh – a dry thing – on psycho-analysis, in which I am rather interested,' he stammered.

He felt hot and embarrassed. He did not like this close proximity with Pamela; added to which his heart had given a queer, uncomfortable jerk when he had heard her use the name 'Julie.' She had called him that in the old days when he had first been her lover. Never since. What on earth was she playing at now? he wondered savagely.

'Psycho-analysis, eh?' murmured Pamela. 'It sounds interesting.'

'Oh – yes – it is.'

'Tell me about it,' said Pamela.

'I'm sorry – it would take much too long to explain,' he said stiffly.

He made a movement as though to rise. But Pamela deliberately put out a hand, caught his arm and held him down in the chair.

'Don't go,' she said in a low, appealing voice. 'You were beastly to me this morning, Julie, but I'll forget that. Be nice to me now. I'm horribly unhappy.'

'I'm sorry,' he said, clearing his throat. His cheeks were red. 'But really, Pamela, I can say or do nothing to comfort you.'

'Can't you?' she whispered.

He knew perfectly well that Pamela was attempting to win him again; using her physical charm and sex-allure in the attempt.

'Pardon me, Pamela,' he said. 'I think I'll go and see if mother is still sleeping.'

'No – don't go!' said Pamela. She held him back in earnest now – both hands gripping his arm. And suddenly she slipped from the chair and went down on her knees before him, looking up at him with big tear-filled eyes. 'Julie, Julie,' she added, her voice breaking, 'how can you be so utterly callous, when once you loved me and made me your wife?'

'Haven't we had all this out?' he asked in despair. 'My dear, you know as well as I do that Stella and I are deeply in love with each other. How can I care for you again? I don't change my affections every five minutes.'

Pamela stretched out both her hands to him.

'Julie – be kind,' she pleaded. 'Try and love me again – oh, do try!'

'Hush, for heaven's sake. My mother is coming,' he said, suddenly springing to his feet. 'She wasn't asleep, after all. And she is coming in here.'

Pamela rose, her breast heaving, her face pale, passionate. She saw Lady Eden moving slowly towards the door, leaning on her ebony stick. And suddenly blind fury swept over her – robbing her of every kind thought – of all decent feeling. She had but one desire – that was to *force* Julian to her side – now that she had failed to win him.

'I shall tell Lady Eden the truth!' she said in a loud, hysterical voice. 'Do you hear me, Julian – I shall tell your mother what she ought to have known years ago!'

'*Pamela*!' said Julian hoarsely, off his guard. 'Be quiet.'

'There you are!' said the girl triumphantly. 'You hear what he calls me, Lady Eden. Pamela! Yes, I *am* Pamela. I am his wife! I am your daughter-in-law! Stella is only an impostor. She has deceived you beautifully, all along. But I'm not going to let it go on. Why should I play second fiddle – take the place of nobody when I am Mrs. Julian Eden and. . . .'

Her voice died away. She had seen an almost murderous gleam in Julian's eyes. She thought for a moment that he would spring at her throat and strangle her. Then she looked swiftly, in a terrified way, at Lady Eden. Julian's agonised face turned to his mother, too. He reached her side just in time to catch her as she fell forward into his arms.

CHAPTER 14

Stella returned from her walk, feeling refreshed and composed. She found the household of Eden Hall in chaos; Lady Eden in bed, with Dr. Bates in attendance, and Julian in a frantic state of anxiety. Pamela was not to be seen.

Julian saw Stella coming up the drive, and ran down to the hall to meet her. The sight of his ashen face roused instant alarm in her.

'My dear – what on earth has happened?' she asked.

'The worst of all things!' he said hoarsely. He gripped her hand and held it in hot, shaking fingers. 'Pamela has told mother . . . *damn her!* . . . yes . . . I can't help saying it . . . I curse the day I ever set eyes on her . . . she has killed mother as sure as fate.'

Stella's heart gave a terrific leap.

'Oh, Julian, Julian, you can't mean it!' she gasped. 'Told mother . . . about us?'

'Yes. And the shock has practically killed mother. She is lying upstairs insensible. Bates is with her and a heart specialist from Southampton has been telephoned for. But Bates gives no hope. He thinks – like I do – that this attack is a fatal one.'

Stella was trembling. She clung to Julian's hand.

'How did it happen? Oh, why did I go out and leave you?' she wailed.

'I wish to God you hadn't gone out!' said Julian. 'Perhaps it wouldn't have happened if you'd been here. Pamela was in a raging temper – she was piqued because I wouldn't respond to her overtures of affection. She drove me to distraction and made me forget myself so that I called her 'Pamela' before mother. Then she turned round and told mother that she *was* Pamela – my real wife, and that you were an impostor. Mother fainted, and she hasn't recovered consciousness since. That was half an hour ago.'

'Good heavens!' said Stella. 'How absolutely awful, Julian! Where is Pamela?'

'I don't know. . . .' Julian bit savagely at his lips. 'I never want to see her again – that's all. I expect she has gone home – back to the hotel – and no doubt she's sorry now for what she's done. It's a wonder I didn't kill her.'

'Oh, hush – you are overwrought, dear,' said Stella, quickly. 'Don't say these terrible things.'

'You know what mother means to me, Stella,' he said in a choked voice.

'I know, darling – but God may spare her even yet. Who knows that she may recover consciousness and remember nothing of what was said.'

'Bates thinks there is a possibility that she may not remember . . . but she will die all the same,' said Julian, in a tone of despair. 'Her heart won't stand this shock. She is sinking rapidly now.'

Stella took off her hat and drew her hand across her eyes.

'Oh, if you knew what I feel!' she said. 'I feel responsible – for it all.'

He put an arm around her.

'No, Stella, don't feel like that. It is not your fault. It is Pamela's.'

'I blame myself,' she said, shaking her head. 'I ought never, never to have come here as your widow. Of course, it's no good regretting things now. It is much too late.'

'Had Pamela kept her temper, things would never have reached this pitch.'

'Ah, they were going this way – all the time. I've only expected this end,' said Stella sadly. 'I didn't see how we could possibly go on with the deception without betraying the truth one day.'

Julian drew her tightly to his side.

'Oh, my dear, my dear,' he said, 'we shall both have need to be brave and strong now. Don't leave me, Stella – stay with me – help me!'

'I shall never leave you while you want me, Julian,' she said earnestly.

He sighed and let her go.

'Let's go upstairs to mother,' he said in a low voice.

They walked across the hall together, As they reached the foot of the stairs the dining-room door opened. A slim, black-clad figure stumbled over the threshold – reached Stella's side – collapsed into Stella's arms.

'Stella – Stella – don't let him turn you against me!' said the hoarse, sob-broken voice of Pamela. 'He hates me – he wants to kill me. Oh, Stella . . . don't turn against me . . . don't!'

Stella stood motionless. Pamela clung wildly to her, sobbing and moaning. Julian looked on with a face like granite.

'Stella,' repeated Pamela, 'put your arms around me – tell me you'll forgive me. Oh, I'm sorry I told Lady Eden – I'm sorry –'

Slowly Stella put her arms around the slender quivering form of the sister whose tears and griefs had been flung at her feet since their childhood; whom she had had to console, to advise, to make sacrifices for all their lives.

For the first time, there was no tenderness in Stella's heart; no love. She knew exactly what Pamela's tears and outbursts of remorse were worth, now. She was beginning to understand how utterly selfish, artificial and shallow Pamela's nature was. Yet she could not wholly ignore this passionate plea for forgiveness – for sympathy. Stella was intensely human and sympathetic. If she could not feel love – she could feel pity.

'My dear,' she said in a sorrowful voice. 'I'm afraid it is too late to say you are sorry, Lady Eden is very, very ill.'

'I know. I'm terribly sorry I told her.'

'Why did you do it?'

'I was angry,' came in a muffled voice. 'I was p-piqued because J-Julian was so horrid.'

'Angry – piqued!' snorted Julian, shaking his head impatiently. 'My God – and because of that you say things you know will hasten a delicate old lady to her death!'

Pamela turned a streaming face to him.

'You've hated me for w-weeks,' she said, sobbing hysterically. 'Now you've got reason to – you're gl-glad!'

'It's not much use making childish remarks like that,' said Stella, rather curtly. 'Pull yourself together please, Pamela. I can't stand here talking to you now. I must go up to Lady Eden.'

'You hate me, too,' said Pamela, drawing away from her sister. 'Julian has t-turned you against me.'

'Not at all. I'm terribly distressed to think you could forget yourself so far as to do what you have done, but Julian has not turned me against you.'

'Oh, he has!' said Pamela in a passionate voice. 'I shall commit suicide. I shall – I shall –'

'Be quiet!' interrupted Stella. 'Be quiet at once! Don't dare say such things! It is wicked and foolish of you, Pamela.'

Pamela dashed the tears from her eyes. Trembling, hysterical, she faced her sister and her husband.

'Well, I'm going away, anyhow,' she said. 'You neither of you want me. I shall run away – never be heard of again.'

Stella turned to Julian.

'What on earth am I to do?' she asked him in a low voice. 'She makes me very anxious.'

'Leave her alone,' said Julian. 'She'll get over it. Let her go away if she wants to.'

Stella gave a sharp sigh. She turned back to Pamela; held out her hand.

'Try to control yourself, Pam,' she said. 'I can't stay and talk to you now. I must go up to Julian's mother. You have done enough harm; for heaven's sake don't do any more. Be reasonable and keep calm and quiet for a little while until I can come and talk things over with you. Wait for me down here.'

'No – I shan't – I shall run away!' panted the other girl. 'You'll never see me again!'

'Don't take any notice of her. It is pure hysteria,' said Julian, taking Stella's arm. 'Come, dear – I want you upstairs, in case mother recovers consciousness.'

Pamela cast him a look of undisguised hatred, then turned and ran out of the house. Stella wanted to run after her, but Julian begged her to go with him.

'It's only temper. She won't do any harm,' he said. 'Mother needs you more than Pamela does. Come with me, Stella – Pamela will be all right. She'll probably go to the hotel and find Arthur. She's been getting on the right side of him the last day or two. That's where she'll go. I'll stake a good deal on it.'

'She's so passionate and foolish,' said Stella, her voice breaking. 'Oh, what is going to be the end of it all? I feel absolutely bewildered, Julian.'

He put an arm about her – drew her upstairs toward his mother's bedroom.

'You poor darling,' he murmured. 'It's enough to upset anybody. I feel like hell, myself!'

Bates met them outside Lady Eden's door.

'Glad you've come up,' he said brusquely. 'Lady Eden's just coming round, and asking for you . . .' he nodded at Julian.

'Is she all right?'

'I can't say that. She's pretty feeble. I shall be glad when Charteris comes. He ought to be here by now. He has a very powerful car.

'I hear a car coming up the drive now' said Stella, 'I expect that is Dr. Charteris.'

She turned and walked downstairs again to meet the specialist.

Julian tiptoed into his mother's room and knelt down by the bed, looking anxiously at her. Her delicate face was pinched. It seemed to have become smaller since her sudden attack. Her lips were ominously blue, and her breathing laboured. Her eyes were open now. They looked up into Julian's face, fixedly.

'Julian,' she said, her voice scarcely audible.

'Mother, darling, I'm here – yes?' he answered, taking her hand in his.

'Julian – I – what has – happened?' came the faint query.

'Nothing, darling. You've just had a heart-attack – like you've had before. You'll be quite all right soon. Bates is here, and Dr Charteris is coming to see you.'

'It – isn't – like my other attacks,' she said, closing her eyes. 'I – think I'm – dying, Julian.'

'No, no!' he said, his face contracting. 'Dearest, you aren't going to die – of course you're not!'

'But what – happened?' she persisted. 'I – have I been – dreaming, Julian . . . bad dreams? About you . . . Stella . . . Pamela . . . ah . . . that's it . . . Stella . . . what did she say when . . . '

'Nothing, darling,' Julian broke in. He was determined at all costs to spare his mother from the truth. If she were to die – she must die happy – in ignorance of the facts. She did not, obviously, remember exactly what Pamela had said . . . he would assure her she had been dreaming.

'There is nothing for you to worry about, Mother,' he said clearly, bending over her. 'When you fainted in the drawing-room, Stella was with us – and I called her "Pamela" by mistake. Don't you remember – we were just laughing about it – and you – you fainted.'

Lady Eden's brows drew together . . . her lips moved . . . the frail hand in Julian's was twitching.

'Did I? Yes. . . . I do remember . . . you called Stella "Pamela" . . . but she said . . . she said she *was* Pamela

. . . I . . .'

'No – dearest – what nonsense! You have been dreaming,' said Julian. He prayed to be forgiven for the lie he had uttered.

Lady Eden opened her eyes again.

'Perhaps I – was dreaming,' she said with difficulty. 'Oh, Julian . . . I'm so tired!'

He bit his lip and turned round to the doorway. Three people entered the room: Stella, Bates, and Barclay Charteris, the heart-specialist from Southampton. The latter was a tall, grey-haired man with clever, kindly eyes. Julian rose to his feet and greeted him.

'Thank God you've come,' he said. 'I'm afraid my mother is pretty bad.'

'Let's have a look at her,' said Charteris.

Julian walked to Stella's side. She looked at him with her sweet, compassionate eyes, and took his hand in hers.

'Courage, dear,' she whispered.

He squeezed her fingers so tightly that she winced with pain.

'I've no courage left,' he whispered back. 'This has been a mortal blow to mother. I know it. But she is very hazy about things – she doesn't actually remember what Pam said, so I'm lying like the deuce – and I'm *going* to lie. I want her to die happily – thinking that you are my wife.'

Barclay Charteris was bending over Lady Eden now, taking her pulse and applying the stethoscope. He was not long in his examination. He laid down the instrument and drew Bates aside. They whispered together for a moment, then came across to Julian and Stella.

One glance at Charteris' face told Julian the worst.

'She is dying?' he asked in a hoarse undertone.

'I'm afraid there is no hope, my boy,' said the specialist gravely. 'The shock – whatever it is – has been too much for her. She is sinking fast.'

Julian held on to Stella.

'How – long?' he managed to ask.

'A matter of moments,' was the reply.

Julian set his teeth.

'I shall curse Pamela to my dying day for this,' he said.

'If it is any consolation to you, my dear chap,' said Charteris, 'your mother could not have lived many weeks in any case – with or without a shock. Her heart was in a very precarious state, from what Bates tells me.'

Lady Eden called to her son.

'Julian. . . . '

The faint whisper brought him at once to her side, and Stella went with him. The old lady looked up at them both. Her blue-tinged lips curved into a tender smile.

'My dear – ones,' she gasped.

Charteris, at the other side of the bed, administered a stimulant. Momentarily it gave Lady Eden the strength she required to make what was to be her last speech on earth.

'Julian – Pamela!' she said quite clearly. 'Are you sure – I have been dreaming? You – you two *are* married – aren't you?'

'Of course,' said Julian.

'Of course, dear,' echoed Stella. 'Married and wonderfully happy – you know that.'

Lady Eden's smile broadened. She closed her eyes.

'Bless you – both . . . ' she murmured.

And then suddenly a look of terrible agony convulsed her features. She fell back on her pillow, gasping piteously for breath.

'Oh, my God!' said Julian. 'Charteris – save her – don't let her go –'

But Charteris could do no more. Lady Eden was beyond human aid. The look of pain passed. Her face was peaceful, contented, now. But she no longer breathed.

Julian gave one anguished look at the marble white face of the mother he had worshipped; then turned to Stella.

'She's – dead, Stella,' he said brokenly.

'She died quite happily, darling,' said the girl, her face bathed in tears. 'She did not know the truth. We can at least be thankful for that.'

Julian stumbled on to his feet and walked from the room. Nobody followed him. It was best to leave him alone with his grief.

But Stella knelt beside the body of the woman whom she had deceived to the very end, and wept, heart-brokenly and bitterly.

It was all over . . . all the need for lies, for deception – for planning and plotting to keep the truth from Julian's idolised mother. Their lips were no longer sealed. In a measure, it was a great burden lifted from them. But it was also a never-ending sorrow. For the dead cannot be recalled and they had both loved Lady Eden with all their hearts.

And now, what of the future?

Stella dared not begin to think.

Tea-time had come and gone. Nobody bothered about the meal. Nobody wanted to eat or drink. Julian had been shut in his study, refusing to admit anybody – even Stella – since his mother's death; and now, when dusk crept through the gardens and filled the house with violet shadows – everything was very quiet. The blinds were drawn at all the windows. The flag which usually fluttered so gaily in the breeze, from the highest turret of Eden Hall, was at half-mast.

Bates and Charteris had, of course, departed. There was nothing more for them to do. The servants – including Hannah, who had loved and faithfully served Lady Eden for many years – clustered in the servants' hall – weeping for their lost mistress.

Stella was the only active person in the house. She felt unable to sit down quietly and give way to her sorrow. There was much to do – much to arrange. And now that Lady Eden was no more, the thought of Pamela worried Stella terribly. She felt she must go to the 'Crown' and see what had happened to the girl who had left the house in such a state of hysteria and nerves.

It was a long way from the village to Eden Hall, and she was much too tired to walk. She decided to take Julian's two-seater. She knew how to drive. That was one of the things Julian had taught her since she had lived here as his wife.

She put on her coat and hat and walked to the garage. A few minutes later she was driving swiftly through the fast-deepening twilight, toward Lyndhurst.

She reached the 'Crown,' asked for Mrs Raynes, and learned, to her dismay, that Pamela was no longer there.

'Mrs Raynes left Lyndhurst for London this afternoon,' the girl at the bureau informed her.

'And Major Lucas?'

'He went with Mrs Raynes, Madam.'

Astonished and perplexed, Stella stood in the lounge a moment, wondering what next to do. Her mind was a blank. She had counted on seeing Pam and discussing the future. And Pam had left Lyndhurst . . . with Lucas! What did it all mean?

'Mrs Raynes left a note for you,' the reception-clerk informed her the next minute. 'I'm sorry – I forgot it when you first asked for her.'

Stella took the letter eagerly. Perhaps this would explain. She ripped open the envelope and scanned the few lines which Pamela had written in her untidy, scrawling hand.

'Dear Stella,

After all that has happened to-day I feel I cannot possibly remain in Lyndhurst. I expect Lady Eden will die and Julian will blame me for her death. I'm going to London to an hotel until I decide what next to do. Major Lucas is very sorry for me – he is the only one who understands how miserable I am. You and Julian think only of yourselves.

'Good-bye,

'Pamela.'

Slowly Stella folded up this note (so typical of Pamela) and placed it in her pocket. Then she walked out to the car, started the engine, and drove back to Eden Hall. Her sweet face was a trifle flushed.

She considered it grossly unfair of Pamela to have acted in this way, and to accuse her and Julian of thinking 'only of themselves.' It was not so. They had considered her a great deal. But, after all, she had caused Lady Eden's sudden death, and she was to blame in a great measure for much of the sorrow and trouble which had recently befallen them all.

And Lucas had gone with Pamela . . . he was sorry for her . . . understood how miserable she was. . . .

Stella compressed her lips.

'H'm,' she thought. 'So Pamela had enlisted Major Lucas on to her side. I wonder if he would be sorry for her if he knew just what she is like?'

There was no love left in Stella's heart for her sister. By her own actions Pamela had wiped out that once absorbing affection. How could anybody love a girl so utterly selfish and inconsequent as Pamela had proved herself to be this last year?

And now, what was going to happen? They were all in as great a muddle as ever. Pamela was still legally Julian's wife. She, Stella, was nothing; had no rightful place in Eden Hall.

'I shall have to go away,' Stella told herself wretchedly. 'There is nothing else for me to do.'

She could not remain at Eden Hall as Julian's wife now that Lady Eden was dead. It was impossible.

When she reached home she found Julian in the library. He was smoking a cigarette, standing before the fireplace. He looked ravaged by grief; his face colourless, his eyes rimmed with red.

Stella, who loved him so, and who was soon to leave him for ever, felt her heart go out to him. She walked up to him, surrendering her hands to his.

'Oh, my dear – my dear!' she said.

He threw away his cigarette and took her in his arms. He laid his face against her soft neck, sighing deeply.

'Darling,' he said. 'I have only you now – only you!

Her features contracted. In silence a moment she stroked his head. Then she said:

'Sit down on the sofa with me, Julian, darling. There is so much to be said.'

He closed his eyes – and opened them again with another long sigh.

'Yes, I suppose there is. But I can't think of anything at the moment except that I – have lost mother.'

'My poor, poor boy!' said Stella, pressing her lips to his cheek. 'How can I possibly comfort you?'

'Who can if you can't!' he said with emotion.

She could feel his strong body shaking. Afraid that he was going to break down again, she kept a stiff upper-lip, herself. She drew him down on to the sofa beside her, and keeping her arms about him, began to speak to him in a quiet voice.

'Julian, we must talk things over very calmly,' she said. 'I have just been to the 'Crown,' and Pamela has gone.'

'Gone where?' he asked dully.

'To London. She left this note.'

Julian read the letter. His lips curled a little as he returned it to Stella.

'So Arthur has taken her back to town, has he? What a fool! She's caught him, I suppose.'

'Oh, I don't know about that,' said Stella, her face burning. 'But he seems to be sorry for her.'

'I'm glad she's got somebody to pity her. I never want to look upon her face again,' he muttered.

'She is still your wife, Julian.'

'No. You are my wife – my real wife!' he said in a passionate voice. He drew her closely to him and smoothed the silky dark hair back from her brow. He kissed her on the mouth twice, slowly, lingeringly. '*You* are my wife, Stella,' he repeated.

She shivered and turned her face to him. She yearned to respond to his kisses, but she knew she must not lose her self-control now. She must be strong and do the right thing at last. For weeks she had done wrong – acted her part gladly because of Lady Eden. But now there was no excuse. She must no longer pretend to be Julian's wife.

Gently she drew away from his arms.

'My dearest,' she said, 'you know that I love you. But you know, also, that I am *not* your wife. I must go away – directly after the – the funeral.'

He caught at her blindly – buried his face on her breast.

'Stella, Stella, don't leave me,' he said. 'I shall go mad if I have to lose you as well as mother.'

'Oh, my darling,' she said, torn between her love and her duty,' how can I stay? Pamela is your wife and as long as that tie exists, how can I, her sister, remain with you? Julian, try to see reason – for my sake. Don't – *don't* cry, darling, or *I* shall go mad!'

She could feel his tears soaking through her thin frock – scalding her bosom. It nearly broke her heart. She held him to her with tender, straining arms, kissing his head again and again.

'Be brave – be brave, my love,' she kept on saying. 'I must leave you. You know that I must. Don't try to keep me. It would be wrong.'

Gradually Julian recovered his lost balance. But he was still shaking. He felt desolate – hopeless.

But after two hours talk with Stella, he was bound to agree with her. She could not stay in Eden Hall now. Pamela was his wife. Pamela stood between them. Unless Pamela agreed to dissolve that union – which apparently she would not do – Stella could never belong to him.

They looked at each other – hollow-eyed – hopeless. The next minute they were in each other's arms – their lips locked in a kiss of the most poignant and passionate love.

'Never again, my darling,' said Julian hoarsely, as he held her. 'Never again! This must be good-bye. . . .'

Two days later the body of Cecily Eden was laid to rest in the Eden vault, in the quiet little cemetery of the church at Lyndhurst.

After the funeral, which had been attended only by Lady Eden's son and the girl who had posed as his wife, Julian and Stella returned to Eden Hall to settle up final affairs.

They were both unnerved and wretched – thankful that no relatives had come to the funeral, and that now they could be alone. Yet what use to be alone? They must not touch each others hands. That night on which Lady Eden had died, they had bidden each other farewell. They had agreed that it was best that their lips should never meet in another kiss.

Julian was going to make immediate arrangements to close up Eden Hall and leave for the East. And Stella was going to town to find Pamela – Pamela from whom they had not heard a line since that one letter informing them that she had gone to London with Major Lucas.

Lunch was served at one o'clock, but neither Julian nor Stella could eat. They sat opposite each other, toying with the food. Now and then they glanced at each other furtively – almost afraid to let their eyes meet.

Stella looked so pale, so slight in her new mourning, it wrenched Julian's heart to look at her.

Outside, the golden sunshine of summer flooded the lovely gardens of Eden Hall; the birds carolled their joyous songs; the flowers made a riot of colour bordering the cool green of the lawns. Summer, in the fulfilment of her beauty! But Stella felt that Autumn had already come . . . the words of the song she had sung to Julian long ago, reiterated in her mind.

'Summer, Summer, when you fly,
Two of us must say good-bye . . .
Never sunshine, never rain

Will fall on just we two again. . . .'

Burning tears welled into her eyes, and suddenly she felt unable to sit there with the maid's curious eyes upon her – making this poor pretence at eating a meal. She rose, wiped her lips with her serviette, and pushed back her chair.

Julian looked up at her.

'Stella, you've eaten nothing,' he said.

'I – I don't want it,' she stammered.

'Neither do I,' he said shortly. 'We'll go into the drawing-room and have coffee.'

Outside in the hall she faced him, pressing both hands to her breast.

'I think I'd far better go straight to the station now – at once, Julian,' she said hoarsely. 'I can't stand much more of this.'

He set his teeth and moved his head with a gesture of intense pain.

'My dear – I know what you feel. And God knows I'd give the world to be able to take you in my arms and comfort you,' he said.

'You can't – you must not,' she said. 'We must say good-bye, for good. We have agreed upon that.'

'Stella, just come and drink your coffee,' he said in a low tone. 'It will do you good, my poor darling.'

She sighed and followed him into the drawing-room. She wondered how much more anguish she could bear before she gave way – before she flung herself into Julian's arms and begged him to take her abroad – take her, despite everything.

The telephone bell rang sharply, breaking the stillness of the house.

Julian turned back into the hall and picked up the receiver.

'Hullo . . . yes . . . *Pamela* . . . you . . . want Stella . . . yes, hang on . . . ' he turned to Stella. 'It is Pamela, from town,' he added. 'She wants you.'

Stella's heart began to beat swiftly. She took the receiver from Julian and held it to her ear.

'Hullo, Pamela . . . yes . . . *what?* . . . good heavens!'

Julian stood by, smoking a cigarette. He could not guess what Pamela was saying, but it was apparently something astonishing, for Stella's face was flushed and she trembled visibly. He heard her say:

'It doesn't seem right . . . oh, my dear, for God's sake, don't make another mistake!' and then, 'Of course, I hope you will be happy . . . yes, I will tell Julian . . . oh, you mad, mad child!'

And a few minutes later, Stella had hung up the receiver and was clinging to Julian's arm.

'What do you think? Pamela is going away – on the Continent – with Arthur Lucas. She says he is wildly in love with her and only wants to make her happy, and she likes him; she prefers to go with him than live her life alone, as she knows you would never take her back.'

Julian pressed a hand to his head.

'You realise what this means, Stella?' he said. 'It means that I – I can get a divorce!'

He caught her in his arms, held her tightly to his breast, his heart throbbing against her own.

'We need only say good-bye for a little while – not for ever *now,*' he said. When the divorce is through, I shall be able to marry you, Stella – bring you back to Eden Hall again – my wife!'

She closed her eyes and surrendered to his embrace, her arms about his neck.

'Oh, my dear, my dear!' she whispered.

'It will all come right now,' he said, with his lips on her hair. 'Just as mother would have wished it . . . you and I together – always. My love – my beloved – thank God!'

'Thank God,' she echoed.